SAVED BY
THE LIFEBOAT

R.M. BALLANTYNE

Frontispiece by John Betancourt. Based on a painting.

SAVED BY
THE LIFEBOAT

R.M. Ballantyne

WILDSIDE PRESS

SAVED BY
THE LIFEBOAT

INTRODUCTION

Robert Michael Ballantyne (1825–1894) was a Scottish author who published more than 100 books. He was also an accomplished artist and exhibited some of his water-colours at the Royal Scottish Academy.

Ballantyne was born in Edinburgh, the ninth of ten children (and the youngest son), to Alexander and Anne Ballantyne. His father was a newspaper editor and printer in the family firm of "Ballantyne & Co" based at Paul's Works on the Canongate. His uncle, James Ballantyne, was the printer for Scottish author Sir Walter Scott. A banking crisis in 1825 resulted in the collapse of the Ballantyne printing business the following year with debts of £130,000,which led to a decline in the family's fortunes.

Robert Ballantyne went to Canada at the age of 16 and spent five years working for the Hudson's Bay Company. He traded with the local Native Americans for furs, which required him to travel by canoe and sleigh to the areas occupied by the modern-day provinces of Manitoba, Ontario, and Quebec—experiences that formed the basis of his novel *Snowflakes and Sunbeams* (1856). His longing for family and home during that period impressed him to start writing letters to his mother. Ballantyne recalled in his autobiographical *Personal Reminiscences in Book Making* (1893) that "To this long-letter writing I attribute whatever small amount of facility in composition I may have acquired."

In 1847 Ballantyne returned to Scotland to discover that his father had died. He published his first book the following year, *Hudson's Bay: or, Life in the Wilds of North America*, and for some time was employed by the publishers Messrs Constable. In 1856 he gave up business to focus on his literary career and began the series of adventure stories for the young with which his name is popularly associated.

The Young Fur-Traders (1856), *The Coral Island* (1857), *The World of Ice* (1859), *Ungava: a Tale of Eskimo Land* (1857), *The Dog*

Crusoe (1860), *The Lighthouse* (1865), *Fighting the Whales* (1866), *Deep Down* (1868), *The Pirate City* (1874), *Erling the Bold* (1869), *The Settler and the Savage* (1877), and more than 100 other books followed in regular succession, his rule being to write as far as possible from personal knowledge of the scenes he described. *The Gorilla Hunters: A tale of the wilds of Africa* (1861) shares three characters with The Coral Island: Jack Martin, Ralph Rover and Peterkin Gay. Here Ballantyne relied factually on Paul du Chaillu's Exploration in Equatorial Guinea, which had appeared early in the same year.

The Coral Island remains the most popular of the Ballantyne novels still read and remembered today, but because of a mistake he made in that book—he gave an incorrect thickness of coconut shells—he prioritized research on his subjects for later books. For instance, he spent time living with the lighthouse keepers at the Bell Rock before writing *The Lighthouse*, and he spent time with the tin miners of Cornwall while researching *Deep Down*.

In 1866 he married Jane Grant, with whom he had three sons and three daughters. He spent his later years in Harrow, London, before moving to Italy for the sake of his health, possibly suffering from undiagnosed Ménière's disease. He died in Rome in 1894 and was buried in the Protestant Cemetery there.

One of the young men influenced by Ballantyne's novels was Robert Louis Stevenson (1850–94). Stevenson was so impressed with the story of *The Coral Island* (1857) that he based portions of his most famous book, *Treasure Island* (1881), on themes found in Ballantyne's classic novel.

—Karl Wurf
Rockville, Maryland

CHAPTER I.

The Wreck in the Bay.

On a dark November afternoon, not many years ago, Captain Boyns sat smoking his pipe in his own chimney-corner, gazing with a somewhat anxious expression at the fire. There was cause for anxiety, for there raged at the time one of the fiercest storms that ever blew on the shores of England.

The wind was howling in the chimney with wild fury; slates and tiles were being swept off the roofs of the fishermen's huts and whirled up into the air as if they had been chips of wood; and rain swept down and along the ground in great sheets of water, or whirled madly in the air and mingled with the salt spray that came direct from the English Channel; while, high and loud above all other sounds, rose the loud plunging roar of the mighty sea.

"I fear there will be a call before long, Nancy, for the services of the new lifeboat," said Captain Boyns, rising and taking down an oilcloth coat and sou'-wester, which he began to put on leisurely; "I'll go down to the beach and see what's doin' at the Cove."

The captain was a fine specimen of a British sailor. He was a massive man, of iron build, and so tall that his sou'-wester almost touched the ceiling of his low-roofed parlour. His face was eminently masculine, and his usual expression was a compound of sternness, gravity, and good-humour. He was about forty years of age, and, unlike the men of his class at that time, wore a short curly black beard and moustache, which, with his deeply bronzed countenance, gave him the aspect of a foreigner.

"God help those on the sea," said Mrs. Boyns, in reply to her husband's remark; "I'm thankful, Dan, that you are on shore this night."

Nancy was a good-looking, lady-like woman of thirty-three or thereabouts, without anything particularly noteworthy about her. She was busy with her needle at the time we introduce her, and relapsed into silence, while her stalwart husband pulled on a pair of huge sea-boots.

"Did you hear a gun, Nancy?" cried the captain, as a terrific blast shook every timber in the cottage — "there! ain't that it again?"

Nancy listened intently, but could hear nothing save the raging of the storm. The captain completed his toilet, and was about to leave the room when the door suddenly burst open, and a lad of about fourteen years of age sprang in.

"Father," he cried, his eyes flashing with excitement, "there's a brig on the sands, and they are going to launch the new lifeboat!"

"Whereaway is't, lad?" asked Boyns, as he buttoned up his coat.

"To lee'ard of the breakwater."

"Oh Harry, don't be too venturesome," cried Mrs. Boyns earnestly, as her strapping boy was about to follow his father out into the pelting storm.

Harry, who was tall and strong for his age, and very like his father in many respects, turning round with a hearty smile, cried, "No fear, mother," and next instant was gone.

The scene on the beach when father and son reached it was very impressive. So furious was the gale that it tore up sand and gravel and hurled it against the faces of the hardy men who dared to brave the storm. At times there were blasts so terrible that a wild shriek, as if of a storm-fiend, rent the air, and flakes of foam were whirled madly about. But the most awful sight of all was the seething of the sea as it advanced in a succession of great breaking "rollers" into the bay, and churned itself white among the rocks.

Out among these billows, scarce visible in the midst of the conflicting elements, were seen the dark hull, shattered masts, and riven sails of a large brig, over which the waves made clear breaches continually.

In the little harbour of the seaport, which was named Covelly, a number of strong men were engaged in hastily launching a new lifeboat, which had been placed at that station only three weeks before, while, clustering about the pier, and behind every sheltered nook along the shore, were hundreds of excited spectators, not a few of whom were women.

Much earnest talk had there been among the gossips in the town when the lifeboat referred to arrived. Deep, and nautically learned, were the discussions that had been held as to her capabilities, and great the longing for a stiffish gale in order that her powers might be fairly tested in rough weather, for in those days lifeboats were not so numerous as, happily, they now are. Many of the town's-people had only heard of such boats; few had seen, and not one had ever had experience of them. After her arrival the weather had continued tantalisingly calm and fine until the day of the storm above referred to, when at length it changed, and a gale burst forth with such violence that the bravest men in the place shook their heads, and said that no boat of any kind whatever could live in such a sea.

When, however, the brig before referred to was seen to rush helplessly into the bay and to strike on the sands where the seas ran most furiously, all lent a willing hand to launch the new lifeboat into the harbour, and a few men, leaping in, pulled her across to the stairs near the entrance, where a number of seamen were congregated, holding on under the lee of the parapet-wall, and gazing anxiously at the fearful scene outside.

"Impossible!" said one; "no boat could live in such a sea for half a minute."

"The moment she shows her nose outside the breakwater she'll capsize," observed another.

"We'll have to risk it, anyhow," remarked a stout young fellow, "for I see men in the foreshrouds of the wreck, and I, for one, won't stand by and see them lost while we've got a lifeboat by us. Why, wot's the use o' callin' it a lifeboat if it can't do more than other boats?"

As he spoke there came an unusually furious gust which sent a wave right over the pier, and well-nigh swept away one or two of them. The argument of the storm was more powerful than that of the young sailor – no one responded to his appeal, and when the boat came alongside the stairs, none moved to enter her except himself.

"That's right, Bob Gaston," cried one of the four men who had jumped into the boat when she was launched, "I know'd you would be the first."

"And I won't be the last either," said young Gaston, looking back at the men on the pier with a smile.

"Right, lad!" cried Captain Boyns, who came up at the instant and leaped into the boat. "Come, lads, we want four more hands – no, no, Harry," he added, pushing back his son; "your arms are not yet strong enough; come lads, we've no time to lose."

As he spoke, a faint cry was heard coming from the wreck, and it was seen that one of the masts had gone by the board, carrying, it was feared, several poor fellows along with it. Instantly there was a rush to the lifeboat! All thought of personal danger appeared to have been banished from the minds of the fishermen when the cry of distress broke on their ears. The boat was over-manned, and old Jacobs, the coxswain, had to order several of them to go ashore again. In another minute they were at the mouth of the harbour, and the men paused an instant as if to gather strength for the mortal struggle before quitting the shelter of the breakwater, and facing the fury of wind and waves.

"Give way, lads! give way!" shouted old Jacobs, as he stood up in the stern-sheets and grasped the steering oar.

The men bent to the oars with all their might, and the boat leaped out into the boiling sea. This was not one of those splendid boats which now line the shores of the United King-dom; nevertheless, it was a noble craft — one of the good, stable, insubmergible and self-emptying kind which were known as the Greathead lifeboats, and which for many years did good service on our coasts. It sat on the raging waters like a swan, and although the seas broke over it again and again, it rose out of the water buoyantly, and, with the brine pouring from its sides, kept end-on to the seas, surmounting them or dashing right through them, while her gallant crew strained every muscle and slowly urged her on towards the wreck.

At first the men on shore gazed at her in breathless anxiety, expecting every moment to see her overturned and their com-rades left to perish in the waves; but when they saw her reappear from each overwhelming billow, their hearts rose with a rebound, and loud prolonged huzzas cheered the lifeboat on her course. They became silent again, however, when distance and the inter-vening haze of spray and rain rendered her motions indistinct, and their feelings of anxiety became more and more intense as they saw her draw nearer and nearer to the wreck.

At last they reached it, but no one on the pier could tell with what success their efforts were attended. Through the blinding spray they saw her faintly, now rising on the crest of a huge wave, then overwhelmed by tons of water. At last she appeared to get close under the stern of the brig, and was lost to view.

"They're all gone," said a fisherman on the pier, as he wiped the salt water off his face; "I know'd that no boat that ever wos built could live in that sea."

"Ye don't know much yet, Bill, 'bout anything a'most," replied an old man near him. "Why, I've see'd boats in the East, not much better than two planks, as could go through a worse surf than that."

"May be so," retorted Bill, "but I know — hallo! is that her coming off?"

"That's her," cried several voices — "all right, my hearties."

"Not so sure o' that," observed another of the excited band of men who watched every motion of the little craft intently, — "there — why — I do believe there are more in her now than went out in her, what think 'ee, Dick?"

Dick did not reply, for by that time the boat, having got clear of the wreck, was making for the shore, and the observers were all too intent in using their eyes to make use of their tongues. Coming as she did before the wind, the progress of the lifeboat was very different from what it had been when she set out. In a few minutes she became distinctly visible, careering on the crest of the waves towards the harbour mouth, and then it was ascertained beyond doubt that some at least, if not all, of the crew of the brig had been rescued. A short sharp Hurrah! burst from the men on the outlook when this became certain, but they relapsed into deep silence again, for the return of the boat was more critical than its departure had been. There is much more danger in running before a heavy sea than in pulling against it. Every roaring billow that came into the bay near the Cove like a green wall broke in thunder on the sands before reaching the wreck, and as it continued its furious career towards the beach it seemed to gather fresh strength, so that the steersman of the lifeboat had to keep her stern carefully towards it to prevent her from turning broadside on — or, as it is nautically expressed, broaching to. Had she done so, the death of all on board would have been almost inevitable. Knowing this, the men on the pier gazed with breathless anxiety as each wave roared under the boat's stern, lifted it up until it appeared perpendicular; carried it forward a few yards with fearful velocity, and then let it slip back into the trough of the sea.

But the boat was admirably managed, and it was seen, as she drew near, that the steering oar was held in the firm grip of Captain Boyns. On it came before the gale with lightning speed towards the harbour mouth; and here a new danger had to be faced, for the entrance was narrow, and the seas were sweeping not into but athwart it, thereby rendering the danger of being dashed against the pier-end very great indeed.

"Missed it!" burst from several mouths as the boat flew round the head of the breakwater and was overwhelmed by a heavy sea which rendered her for one moment unmanageable, but almost as soon as filled she was again emptied through the discharging tubes in her floor.

"No fear of father missing it," exclaimed young Harry Boyns, with a proud look and flashing eye as he saw the stalwart form of the captain standing firm in the midst of the foam with his breast pressed hard against the steering oar.

"Back your starboard oars! Hold water hard!" shouted several voices.

"She's round! hurrah!" cried Harry, as the boat almost leaped out of the foam and sprang into the comparatively smooth water at the harbour mouth. The rowers gave vent to a short shout of triumph, and several worn, exhausted seamen in the bottom of the boat were seen to wave their hands feebly. At the same time, Captain Boyns shouted in a deep loud voice — "All saved, thank God!" as they swept towards the land.

Then did there arise from the hundreds of people assembled on and near the pier a ringing cheer, the like of which had never been heard before in Covelly. Again and again it was repeated while the lifeboat shot up on the beach, and was fairly dragged out of the sea, high and dry, by many eager hands that were immediately afterwards extended to assist the saved crew of the brig to land.

"Are all saved, father?" asked Harry Boyns, who was first at the side of the boat.

"Ay, lad, every one. Fifteen all told, includin' a woman and a little girl. Lend a hand to get the poor things up to our house, Harry," said the captain, lifting the apparently inanimate form of a young girl over the side as he spoke; "she ain't dead — only benumbed a little with the cold."

Many hands were stretched out, but Harry thrust all others aside, and, receiving the light form of the child in his strong arms, bore her off to his father's cottage, leaving his comrades to attend to the wants of the others.

"Oh Harry!" exclaimed Mrs. Boyns, when her son burst into the house, "is your father safe?"

"Ay, safe and well," he cried. "Look sharp, mother — get hot blankets and things ready, for here's a little girl almost dead with cold. She has just been rescued from a wreck — saved by the new lifeboat!"

CHAPTER II.

Describes a merchant and his god,
and concludes with "a message from the sea."

A close-fisted, hard-hearted, narrow-minded, poor-spirited man was John Webster, Esq., merchant and shipowner, of Ingot Lane, Liverpool. And yet he was not altogether without good points. Indeed, it might be said of him that if he had been reared under more favourable circumstances he might have been an ornament to society and a blessing to his country, for he was intelligent and sociable, and susceptible to some extent of tender influences, when the indulging of amiable feelings did not interfere with his private interests. In youth he had even gone the length of holding some good principles, and was known to have done one or two noble things — but all this had passed away, for as he grew older the hopeful springs were dried up, one by one, by an all-absorbing passion — the love of money — which ultimately made him what he was, a disgrace to the class to which he belonged, and literally (though not, it would seem, in the eye of law) a wholesale murderer!

At first he began by holding, and frequently stating, the opinion that the possession of much money was a most desirable thing; which undoubtedly was — and is, and will be as long as the world lasts — perfectly true, if the possession be accompanied with God's blessing. But Mr. Webster did not even pretend to look at the thing in that light. He scorned to make use of the worldly man's "Oh, of course, of course," when that idea was sometimes suggested to him by Christian friends. On the contrary, he boldly and coldly asserted his belief that "God, if there was a God at all, did not interfere in such matters, and that for his part he would be quite satisfied to let anybody else who wanted it have the blessing if he only got the money." And so it pleased God to give John Webster much money without a blessing.

The immediate result was that he fell in love with it, and, following the natural laws attached to that vehement passion, he hugged it to his bosom, became blind to everything else, and gave himself entirely up to it with a self-denying devotion that robbed him of much of his natural rest, of nearly all his graces, and most of his happiness — leaving him with no hope in this world, save that of increasing his stores of money, and with no hope for the world to come at all.

The abode of Mr. Webster's soul was a dingy little office with dirty little windows, a miserable little fireplace, and filthy little chairs and tables — all which were quite in keeping with the little occupant of the place. The abode of his body was a palatial residence in the suburbs of the city. Although Mr. Webster's soul was little, his body was large — much too large indeed for the jewel which it enshrined, and which was so terribly knocked about inside its large casket that its usual position was awry, and it never managed to become upright by any chance whatever.

To the former abode Mr. Webster went, body and soul, one dark November morning. Having seated himself before his desk, he threw himself back in his chair and began to open his letters — gazing with a placid smile, as he did so, at the portrait of his deceased wife's father — a very wealthy old gentleman — which hung over the fireplace.

We omitted to mention, by the way, that Mr. Webster had once been married. This trifling little event of his life occurred when he was about forty-eight years of age, and was a mercantile transaction of an extremely successful kind, inasmuch as it had brought him, after deducting lawyers' fees, stamps, duties, lost time in courtship, wedding-tour expenses, doctor's fees, deathbed expenses, etc., a clear profit of sixty thousand pounds. To be sure there were also the additional expenses of four years of married life, and the permanent board, lodging, and education of a little daughter; but, all things considered, these were scarcely worth speaking of; and in regard to the daughter – Annie by name – she would in time become a marketable commodity, which might, if judiciously disposed of, turn in a considerable profit, besides being, before she was sold, a useful machine for sewing on buttons, making tea, reading the papers aloud, fetching hats and sticks and slippers, etc. There had, however, been a slight drawback – a sort of temporary loss – on this concern at first, for the piece of goods became damaged, owing to her mother's death having weighed heavily on a sensitive and loving spirit, which found no comfort or sympathy at home, save in the devoted affection of an old nurse named Niven. When Annie reached the age of six years, the doctors ordered change of air, and recommended a voyage to the West Indies. Their advice was followed. Nothing was easier. Mr. Webster had many ships on the sea. These were of two classes. The first class consisted of good, new, well found and manned ships, with valuable cargoes on board which were anxiously watched and longed for; the second class comprised those which were old, worn-out, and unseaworthy, and which, being insured beyond their value, might go to the bottom when they pleased.

One of the best of the first class was selected – the *Water Lily*, A1 on Lloyd's – and in it Annie, with her nurse, was sent to sea for the benefit of her health. The parting was a somewhat important event in Mr. Webster's life, for it convinced him, to his own surprise, that his power to love a human being was not yet utterly gone! Annie's arms clasped convulsively round his neck at the moment of parting – her sobbing "Good-bye, darling papa," had stirred depths which had lain unmoved almost from the days of early manhood. But the memory of this passed away as soon as he turned again to gaze upon the loved countenance of his yellow mistress.

The voyage did Annie much good. The short residence in Demerara, while the vessel was discharging cargo and reloading, wrought wonders, and a letter, forwarded by a ship that sailed a short time after their arrival in "foreign parts," told Mr. Webster that he might expect to see his daughter home again, sound and well, in a month or two at the farthest.

But, to return from this digression to the abode of Mr. Webster's soul: –

Having looked at the portrait of his late wife's father for a moment and smiled, he glanced at the letter in his hand and frowned. Not because he was displeased, but because the writing was cramped and difficult to read. However, the merchant was accustomed to receive such letters from seafaring men on many subjects of interest; he therefore broke the seal and set himself patiently to decipher it. Immediately his countenance became ghastly pale, then it flushed up and became pale again, while he coughed and gasped once or twice, and started up and sat down abruptly. In fact Mr. Webster exhibited all the signs of having received a severe shock, and an eye-witness might have safely concluded that he had just read the news of some great mercantile loss. So it was in one sense – but that was not the ordinary sense.

The letter in question was in the handwriting of a fussy officious "bumble" friend of the wealthy man, who dwelt in the town of Covelly. It ran as follows:

"My dear Sir, —

"I write in great haste, and in much perturbation, having just heard from my servant of the wreck of your ship, the *Water Lily*, in Covelly Bay. She does not seem to be quite sure, however, of the name, and says that the only man who has been rescued is scarcely able to speak, so that I do sincerely hope my domestic, who is a stupid old woman, may turn out to be mistaken. I am on the point of hasting down to the shore to ascertain the truth for myself, but am obliged to write to you this brief and unsatisfactory account of what I have heard, in order to save the post, which is just being closed. You shall hear from me again, of course, by the next mail. — I remain, my dear sir, in much anxiety, your most obedt. humble servant,

"*Joseph Dowler.*"

It chanced that at the moment the above letter was handed to the postmaster, and while the wax was being melted before the final sealing of the post-bag, a sailor lad, drenched to the skin and panting vehemently, dashed into the office.

"Stop! stop!" he cried, "a letter — about the wreck — the *Water Lily* — to the owners — not too late, I hope?"

"No, no, just in time. Here, in with it. There, all right. Now, Jim, off with 'ee."

The postman jumped on his vehicle, the whip cracked, and in another minute the Royal Mail was gone. Thus it came to pass that two epistles reached Mr. Webster that morning from Covelly. But in the extreme agitation of his spirit, he did not observe the other letter which lay among the usual morning mass that still awaited examination. After reading the letter twice, and turning it over with trembling hands, as if he wished there were more in it, he pronounced a deep malediction on his "humble" friend, and rang the bell for his confidential clerk, who was an unusually meek, mild, and middle-aged little man, with a bald head, a deprecatory expression of countenance, and a pen behind his ear.

"Mr. Grinder," said Mr. Webster, putting strong constraint on himself, and pretending to be quite composed, "a letter from Covelly informs me that it is feared the *Water Lily* has been wrecked in — "

"The *Water Lily*, sir!" exclaimed Grinder, starting as if he had received an electric shock.

"I spoke audibly, did I not?" said Mr. Webster, turning with a sharp look on his confidential clerk.

"Ye — s, sir, but, I — Miss An — " The poor man could get no further, being of a timid, nervous temperament, and Mr. Webster, paying no attention to his remark, was going on to say that he intended to go by the mail to Covelly without delay to ascertain the truth for himself, when he was interrupted by the confidential clerk who exclaimed in a burst of agitation —

"There were *two* letters, sir, from Covelly this morning — did you read — "

He stopped, for already his employer had sought for, found, and torn open the second epistle, which was written in a fair, legible hand. It ran thus: —

"*Sir,* —

My father, Captain Boyns, directs me to inform you that your daughter, Miss Annie, has been saved from the wreck of your brig, the *Water Lily*, which ran aground here this afternoon, and has become a total wreck. Your daughter's nurse and the crew have also been rescued by our new lifeboat, which is a noble craft, and, with God's blessing, will yet do good service on this coast. I have pleasure in adding, from myself, that it was my father who rescued your child. She fell into the sea when being passed from the wreck into the boat, and sank, but my father dived and brought her up in safety.

"Much of the brig's cargo has been lost, I regret to say, but a good deal of it has been washed ashore and saved in a damaged state. The captain says that defective compasses were the cause of the disaster. There is not time to give you a more particular account, as it is close upon post-time. Miss Annie sends you her kindest love, and bids me say she is none the worse of what she has passed through. — I am, sir, your obt. servant,

    "Harry Boyns."

"Thank God!" exclaimed Mr. Webster fervently. "Why, what are you staring at, Mr. Grinder?" he added, on observing that his confidential servant was gazing at him with an expression of considerable surprise.

"Excuse me, sir," stammered the unfortunate man, "I — I—in fact — you have so often told me that you did not believe in God that I fancied — I—wondered — "

"Really, Mr. Grinder, I must beg of you to confine your remarks in future entirely to matters of business. The so-called religious observations which you sometimes venture to make in my presence are extremely distasteful, I assure you. In explanation of what I said, however, I may tell you that this letter informs me of my daughter's safety, and I merely used the expression of satisfaction that is usual on such occasions. The phrase, as it is generally understood (except by weak men), commits me to nothing more. But enough of this. I find that the *Water Lily* has indeed been lost. It was fully insured, I believe?"

"Yes, sir, it was."

"Very well; report the matter without delay. I will go to Covelly to-night, and shall probably be back to-morrow."

Saying this, Mr. Webster left the office, and, on the evening of that day, found himself seated in Captain Boyns's parlour, with little Annie on his knee. Her pretty head was on his shoulder, her fair curls straggled over his chest, and her round little arms tightly encircled his large body as far as they could reach, while she sobbed on his bosom and kissed him by turns.

This was quite a new experience in the life of the gold-lover. He had declined to submit to familiar caresses in former years, but on such an occasion as the present, he felt that common propriety demanded the sacrifice of himself to some extent. He therefore allowed Annie to kiss him, and found the operation — performed as she did it — much more bearable than he had anticipated; and when Annie exclaimed with a burst of enthusiasm, "Oh, dear, dear papa, I did feel such a dreadful longing for you when the waves were roaring round us!" and gave him another squeeze, he felt that the market price of the bundle of goods on his knee was rising rapidly.

"Did you think you were going to be drowned, dear?" said Mr. Webster with the air of a man who does not know very well what to say.

"I'm not sure what I thought," replied Annie smiling through her tears. "Oh, I was so frightened! You can't think, papa, how very dreadful it is to see the water boiling all round, and sometimes over you; and such awful thumping of the ship, and then the masts breaking; but what I feared most was to see the faces of the sailors, they were so white, and they looked as if they were afraid. Are men ever afraid, papa?"

"Sometimes, Annie; but a white face is not always the sign of fear — that may be caused by anxiety. Did any of them refuse to obey orders?"

"No; they were very obedient."

"Did any of them get into the lifeboat before you and nurse!"

"Oh, no; they all refused to move till we were put into it, and some of them ran to help us, and were very very kind?"

"Then you may be quite sure they were not afraid, however

pale their faces were; but what of yourself, Annie — were you afraid?"

"Oh, dreadfully, and so was poor nurse; but once or twice I thought of the text that — that — you know who was so fond of, — 'Call upon me in the time of trouble and I will deliver thee,' so I prayed and felt a little better. Then the lifeboat came, and, oh! how my heart did jump, for it seemed just like an answer to my prayer. I never felt any more fear after that, except when I fell into the sea; but even then I was not so frightened as I had been, for I felt somehow that I was sure to be saved, and I was right, you see, for dear Captain Boyns dived for me. I love Captain Boyns!" cried Annie, and here again she kissed her father and held him so tight that he felt quite angry with Mrs. Niven, who entered at the moment, and said, apologetically —

"Oh! la, sir, I didn't know as Miss Annie was with you. I only came to say that everythink is ready, sir, for going 'ome."

"We don't intend to go home," said Mr. Webster; "at least not for a day or two. I find that Captain Boyns can let us stay here while I look after the wreck, so you can go and arrange with Mrs. Boyns."

During the few days that Mr. Webster remained at Coral Cottage (Captain Boyns's residence), Mrs. Niven found, in the quiet, sympathetic Mrs. Boyns, if not a congenial friend, at least a kind and sociable hostess, and Annie found, in Harry Boyns, a delightful companion, who never wearied of taking her to the cliffs, the shore, and all the romantic places of the neighbour-hood, while Mr. Webster found the captain to be most serviceable in connection with the wreck. One result of all this was that Mr. Webster offered Captain Boyns the command of one of his largest vessels, an offer which was gladly accepted, for the captain had, at that time, been thrown out of employment by the failure of a firm, in the service of which he had spent the greater part of his nautical career.

Another result was, that Mr. Webster, at Annie's earnest solicitation, agreed to make Covelly his summer quarters next year, instead of Ramsgate, and Mrs. Boyns agreed to lodge the family in Coral Cottage.

This having been all settled, Mr. Webster asked Captain Boyns, on the morning of his departure for Liverpool, if he could do anything more for him, for he felt that to him his daughter owed her life, and he was anxious to serve him.

"If you could give my son Harry something to do, sir," said Boyns, "you would oblige me very much. Harry is a smart fellow and a good seaman. He has been a short time in the coasting trade; perhaps — "

"Well, yes, I'll see to that," interrupted Mr. Webster. "You shall hear from me again as to it."

Now the fact is that Mr. Webster did not feel attracted by young Boyns, and he would willingly have had nothing to do with him, but being unable to refuse the request after having invited it, he ultimately gave him a situation in one of his coasting vessels which plied between London and Aberdeen.

About a year after that, Captain Boyns sailed in the *Warrior*, a large new ship, for the Sandwich Islands and the Chinese seas.

True to his promise, Mr. Webster spent the following summer with Annie and Mrs. Boyns at Covelly, and young Boyns so managed matters that he got his captain to send him down to Covelly to talk with his employer on business. Of course, being there, it was natural that he should ask and obtain leave to spend a few days with his mother; and, of course, it was quite as natural that, without either asking or obtaining leave, he should spend the whole of these days in roaming about the shore and among the cliffs with Annie Webster.

It would be absurd to say that these two fell in love, seeing that one was only seven and the other fifteen; but there can be no doubt they entertained some sort of regard for each other, of a very powerful nature. The young sailor was wildly enthusiastic, well educated, manly, and good-looking — little wonder that Annie liked him. The child was winning in her ways, simple, yet laughter-loving, and very earnest — less wonderful that Harry liked *her*!

Another year fled, and again the Websters visited Covelly, and again Harry spent a few days with his mother; and although Mr. Webster did not get the length of liking the youth, he at last came to the condition of not disliking him.

Year followed year, and still, each summer, Annie pressed her father to return to the old place, and he agreed, chiefly because it mattered little to him where he went. He regarded the summer trip in the light of a penance to be paid for the sin of being a member of society and the head of a household, and placed every minute so wasted to the debit of the profit and loss account in the mental ledger of his life's affairs, for it must not be supposed that Mr. Webster's character was changed by the events which followed the rescue of his child from the sea. True, he had been surprised out of his habitual hardness for a short time, but he soon relapsed, if not quite back to the old position, at least so near to it that the difference was not appreciable.

As time ran on, men begun to look for the return of the *Warrior*, but that vessel did not make her appearance. Then they began to shake their heads and to grow prophetic, while those who were most deeply interested in the human beings who manned her became uneasy.

"Don't fret over it," said Harry one day to his mother, in a kind, earnest tone; "you may depend upon it father will turn up yet and surprise us. He never lost a ship in his life, and he has sailed in worse ones than the *Warrior* by a long way."

"It may be so," replied Mrs. Boyns, sadly; "but it is a long, long time since he went away. God's will be done. Whether He gives or takes away, I shall try to bless His name."

At last Harry gave over attempting to comfort his mother, for he began to fear that his father's ship was destined to be placed on the dark, dreary list of those of which it is sometimes said, with terrible brevity, in the newspapers, "She sailed from port on such and such a day, and has not since been heard of."

In course of time Harry made one or two trips to the East Indies as first mate of one of Mr. Webster's vessels, and ultimately obtained the command of one.

At last a day came when there appeared in a Welsh newspaper a paragraph, which ran thus: — "A Message from the Sea — A bottle, corked and sealed, was found by a woman on the beach, above Conway, North Wales. Inside was a letter containing the following: —

"'Lat. 44, long. 15, off Tierra del Fuego. If this should ever reach the shores of England, it will announce to friends at home the sad fate of the ship *Warrior*, which sailed from Liverpool on 13th February 18 — , bound for China. We have been boarded by pirates: we have been all locked into the cabin, with the assurance that we shall be made to walk the plank in half an hour. Our last act is to put this in a bottle and drop it overboard. Farewell, for this world, my beloved wife and son.'

"*Daniel Boyns*, Captain.'"

This letter was forwarded to the owner, and by him was sent to poor Mrs. Boyns.

Alas! how many sailors' wives, in our sea-girt isle, have received similar "messages from the sea," and lived under the dark cloud of never-ending suspense — hoping against hope that the dear lost ones might yet return!

CHAPTER III.

Shows what some men will do and dare for money,
and what sometimes comes of it.

We must now beg the reader's permission to allow a few more years to elapse. Eight have come and gone since the dark day when poor Mrs. Boyns received that message from the sea, which cast a permanent cloud over her life. Annie Webster has become a beautiful woman, and Harry Boyns a bronzed stalwart man.

But things have changed with time. These two seldom meet now, in consequence of the frequent absence of the latter on long voyages, and when they do meet, there is not the free, frank intercourse that used to be. In fact, Mr. Webster had long ago begun to suspect that his daughter's regard for the handsome young sailor was of a nature that bade fair to interfere with his purposed mercantile transactions in reference to her, so he wisely sent him off on voyages of considerable length, hoping that he might chance to meet with the same fate as his father, and wound up by placing him in command of one of his largest and most unseaworthy East Indiamen, in the full expectation that both captain and vessel would go to the bottom together, and thus enable him, at one stroke, to make a good round sum out of the insurance offices, and get rid of a troublesome servant!

Gloating over these and kindred subjects, Mr. Webster sat one morning in his office mending a pen, and smiling in a sardonic fashion to the portrait of his deceased wife's father, when a tap came to the door, and Harry Boyns entered.

"I have come, sir," he said, "to tell you that the repairs done to the *Swordfish* are not by any means sufficient. There are at least — "

"Please do not waste time, Captain Boyns, by entering upon details," said Mr. Webster, interrupting him with a bland smile: "I am really quite ignorant of the technicalities of shipbuilding. If you will state the matter to Mr. Cooper, whom I employ expressly for — "

"But, sir," interrupted Harry, with some warmth, "I *have* spoken to Mr. Cooper, and he says the repairs are quite sufficient."

"Well, then, I suppose they are so."

"I assure you, sir," rejoined Harry, "they are not; and as the lives of passengers as well as men depend upon the vessel being in a seaworthy condition, I do trust that you will have her examined by some one more competent to judge than Mr. Cooper."

"I have no doubt of Mr. Cooper's competence," returned Mr. Webster; "but I will order a further examination, as you seem so anxious about it. Meanwhile I hope that the ship is being got ready for sea as quickly as possible."

"There shall be no delay on my part, sir," said Harry, rising; "the ship has been removed from the Birkenhead Docks, in which you are aware she has lain for the last eight months, and is now lying in the Brunswick Dock, taking in cargo. But I think it a very serious matter, which demands looking into, the fact that she had no sooner grounded in the dock, than she sprang a leak which instantly let twenty-eight inches of water into her, and twice, subsequently, as much as forty inches have been sounded. Yet no repairs worthy of the name have been made. All that has been done is the pumping of her out daily by the stevedore's men when their stowing work is finished."

"Has the agent for the underwriters visited her?" inquired Mr. Webster.

"He has, sir, but he seems to be of opinion that his responsibility is at an end because a surveyor from the Mersey Docks and Harbour Board had previously visited her, and directed that she should not be loaded deeper than twenty-one feet — chalking on the side amidships the six feet six inches clear beneath which she is not to be allowed to sink."

"Well, well," said Mr. Webster, somewhat impatiently, "I will have the matter looked into. Good morning, Captain Boyns."

The captain bowed and left the office, and Mr. Webster leant back in his chair, clasped his hands, twirled his thumbs, and smiled grimly at the old gentleman over the fireplace.

True to his word, however, he had an inspection made of the *Swordfish*. The inspector was of a kindred spirit with Mr. Webster, so that his report was naturally similar to that of Mr. Cooper. Nothing, therefore, was done to the vessel — "nothing being needed" — and the loading went on in spite of the remonstrances of Captain Harry Boyns, who, with all the energy and persistency of his character, continued to annoy, worry, and torment every one who possessed the faintest right or power to interfere in the matter — but all to no purpose; for there are times when neither facts nor fancies, fair words nor foul, fire, fury, folly, nor philosophy, will avail to move some "powers that be!"

In a towering fit of indignation Harry Boyns resolved to throw up his situation; but it occurred to him that this would perhaps be deemed cowardice, so he thought better of it. Then he madly thought of going direct to the President of the Board of Trade and making a solemn protest, backed by a heart-stirring appeal; but gave up that idea on recalling to memory a certain occasion on which a deputation of grave, learned, white-haired gentlemen had gone to London expressly to visit that august functionary of the State, and beseech him, with all the earnestness that the occasion demanded, that he would introduce into Parliament a bill for the better regulation and supervision of ships, and for preventing the possibility of seamen and passengers being seduced on board unseaworthy vessels, carried off to sea, and there murderously drowned in cold blood, as well as in cold water; which deputation received for answer, that "it was not the intention of Government, as at present advised, to introduce a measure for providing more stringent enactments as to the equipments, cargoes, and crews of passenger vessels!" — a reply which was tantamount to saying that if the existing arrangements were inadequate to the ends desired, Government saw no way out of the difficulty, and people must just be left unprotected, and go to sea to be drowned or spared according as chance or the cupidity of shipowners might direct!

This was pretty resolute on the part of Government, considering that above a thousand lives were then, and above two thousand still are, lost annually on the shores of the United Kingdom; a very large number of which — if we may believe the argument of facts and the pretty unanimous voice of the press — are sacrificed because Government refuses to interfere effectively with the murderous tendencies of a certain class of the community!

When Harry Boyns thought of all this he sighed deeply, and made up his mind to remain by the *Swordfish*, and sink or swim with her. Had he been more of a man of business, perhaps he might have been more successful in finding out how to have prevented the evil he foresaw; but it was the interest of the owner to keep him in the dark as much as possible, for which end Mr. Webster kept him out of the ship's way as much as he could, and when that was impossible, he kept him so busily employed that he remained ignorant of a great deal that was said and done in regard to his vessel.

At length the *Swordfish* left the Brunswick Dock, *six inches deeper* than the surveyor had directed, and was towed to the Wellington Dock, where she took in 120 tons of coke, and sank still deeper. Harry also discovered that the equipment of the ship was miserably insufficient for the long voyage she was intended to make. This was too much for him to bear. He went at once to Mr. Webster's office and said that if a deaf ear was to be turned any longer to his remonstrances he would throw up his appointment.

Poor Harry could scarcely have taken a more effective step to insure the turning of the deaf ear to him.

"Oh!" replied Mr. Webster, coolly, "if you refuse to take charge of my vessel, Captain Boyns, I will soon find another to do it."

"I certainly do refuse," said Harry, preparing to leave the office, "and I think you will find some difficulty in getting any other man to go to sea in such a ship."

"I differ from you, Captain Boyns. Good afternoon."

"And if you do, and lives should be lost in consequence," added Harry, grasping the handle of the door, "I warn you solemnly, that murder will have been committed by you, whatever the law may say on the subject."

"Good afternoon, Captain Boyns."

"You've got a hard master," said Harry to Grinder as he passed through the outer office.

The confidential clerk shook his head in a deprecatory way, and smiled.

Next moment Harry Boyns found himself in the street — with nothing to do, and the wide world before him!

Meanwhile, the loading of the *Swordfish* went on — also the pumping of her. That same day she was visited by a surveyor from the Underwriters' Association, who found her only five feet clear above water, and still taking in cargo. That gentleman called in another surveyor to a consultation, who agreed with him in pronouncing her overladen. She was represented as such to the local Underwriters' Association for which the surveyor acted, but as the *Swordfish* was insured in London and not with them, the Liverpool underwriters did not consider themselves called upon to interfere. Their surveyor, however, visited the vessel again, a few days later, when he found her "only four feet clear," and declared that, so far from going to Bombay, he should not like to attempt to cross to Dublin in her in anything like rough weather.

Now it must be observed that all these consultations and investigations took place in a quiet way. To the public eye all was "fair and above board." Few among the thousands who visited the docks knew much about deep loading; still less about adequate equipping. They saw nought but a "noble ship," well painted, washed, gilded, and varnished, taking merchandise into her insatiable hold, while the "Yo-heave-ho" of the seamen rang out cheerily to the rattling accompaniment of chains and windlass. Many other ships were there, similarly treated, equally beautiful, and quite as worthy of the titles "good" and "noble" as the whited sepulchre is to be styled pure.

A few days before the *Swordfish* was ready for sea, a new captain was sent down to her. This captain was not a "bad man" in the worst sense of that term — neither was he a "good" one. Vigour, courage, resolution when acting in accordance with his inclinations — these were among his characteristics. But he was a reckless man, in want of money, out of employment, and without an appreciable conscience. In the circumstances, he was glad to get anything to do, and had been so long ashore and "in trouble," that he would probably have agreed to take command of and go to sea in a washing-tub if part paid beforehand for doing so.

Nevertheless, even this man (Captain Phelps by name) felt some degree of nervous anxiety on getting on board and examining the state of the ship. On further acquaintance with her, he was so dissatisfied that he also resolved to throw up his appointment. But he had obtained the berth through the influence of a friend who happened to be acquainted with Mr. Webster. This "friend" wrote him a stern letter, saying, if he ventured to do as he proposed, he should never have a ship out of Liverpool again, as long as he (the friend?) could prevent it!

Captain Phelps was one of those angry men of iron mould, who appear to take pleasure in daring Fate to do her worst. On receipt of the letter, he swore with an awful oath that he would now go to sea in the *Swordfish*, even if he knew she would go to the bottom in twenty-four hours after weighing anchor. Accordingly, having intrenched himself behind a wall of moral adamant, he went about with quiet indifference, and let things take their course. He made no objection whatever when, in addition to the loading already in the ship, the agents added a deck cargo of some massive pieces of machinery, weighing thirty tons, and a supply of coals, the proper receptacle for which below had been filled with iron goods. Neither did he utter a word when — after the vessel had been taken out into the stream by the riggers — he and the owner, agents, pilot, and crew (only six of which last were A.B.s), were taken off to her in a tug and put on board with orders to sail immediately.

Only a few passengers were going. These were already on board, but some of their friends went off in the tug to bid them a last farewell.

This was a sad scene, but the captain regarded it with stoical indifference. There was a stout, hale old Indian officer going out on a pleasure trip to his beloved East, and a daughter of the same whom he hoped to get married "offhand, comfortably there."

There was a sick nephew of the old officer, going the voyage for the benefit of his health, on whose wan countenance consumption, if not death, had evidently set a deep mark. There were, also, a nurse and a lady's-maid, and two girls of ten or thirteen years of age — sisters — who were going to join their father and mother, besides one or two others. Earnest loving words passed kindly between these and their relatives and friends as the moment of parting drew near.

"Don't forget to remember me to Coleman and the rest of 'ours,'" cried a stout elderly man, waving his hand as the tug moved off.

"That I won't, and I shall expect to shake you by the hand again, old fellow, in a year or two."

"You'll never see him again," thought Captain Phelps, as he stood with compressed lip and frowning eye on the quarter-deck.

"Good-bye, darling Nelly," cried a lady to one of the sobbing girls from whom she was parting; "remember the message to mamma."

"Oh! yes," exclaimed the child, trying to look bright, "and we won't be very long of coming back again."

"You'll never come back again," thought the captain, and he sighed *very* slightly as the thought passed through his brain.

"Look alive there, lads," exclaimed the pilot, as the tug sheared away.

Soon the anchor was at the bows, the sails were shaken out, and the *Swordfish* began her voyage.

"There's not a piece of spare rope aboard, sir," said the first mate, coming up to the captain with a blank look; "we can't even get enough to cat and fish the anchor."

"You can unreeve the tops'l halyards," replied the captain, quietly.

This was done, and the anchor was secured therewith.

"How much water in the hold?" asked the captain.

"Three feet, sir; the carpenter has just sounded. It seems that the riggers were at work on the pumps when we came out in the tug, but were stopped by the agents before we got alongside. I fear she is very leaky, sir," said the mate.

"I *know* she is," replied the captain; "keep the men at the pumps."

That night the weather became what sailors call "dirty," and next morning it was found that the water had mounted to 4 feet 10 inches. The pumps had become almost unworkable, being choked with sand, and it became evident that the voyage thus inauspiciously begun would very soon be ended. During the day the "dirty" weather became gale, so that, although the wind was fair, Captain Phelps determined to run to the nearest port for shelter. With a "good ship" this might have been done easily enough — many a vessel does it during every gale that visits our stormy shores — but the *Swordfish* was by this time getting water-logged and unmanageable. She drifted helplessly before the gale, and the heavy seas broke over her continually, sweeping away everything moveable. Another night passed, and next morning — Sunday — it became plain that she was settling down so the captain gave orders to get out the long-boat, and told the passengers to get ready. Day had broken some time before this, but the weather was still so thick that nothing could be seen.

"Take a cast of the lead," said the captain.

"Ay, ay, sir," was the prompt reply, but before the order could be obeyed, the roar of breakers was heard above the howling of the storm, and the shout, "Land on the port bow!" was instantly followed by "Down with the helm!" and other orders hurriedly given by the captain and hastily obeyed by the men. All too late! The ship was embayed. As if to make their position more painful, the mists cleared partially away, and revealed the green fields and cottages on shore, with the angry sea — an impassable caldron of boiling foam — between.

Another instant and the ship struck with a convulsive quiver from stem to stern. The billows flew madly over her, the main-mast went by the board — carrying two of the men to their doom along with it — and the *Swordfish*, "bound for Bombay," was cast, a total wreck, upon the coast of Cornwall.

CHAPTER IV.

The Rescue.

Fortunate is it for this land that those who war for evil and those who fight for good do so side by side; and well is it for poor humanity that the bane and the antidote grow together. The misanthrope sends his poisonous streams throughout the land, but the philanthropist erects his dams everywhere to stem the foul torrents and turn them aside. The Infidel plants unbelief with reckless hand far and wide, but the Christian scatters the "Word" broadcast over the land. The sordid shipowner strews the coast with wreck and murdered fellow-creatures; but, thank God, the righteous shipowner — along with other like-minded men — sends forth a fleet of lifeboats from almost every bay and cove along the shore to rob the deep of its prey, and rescue the perishing.

In the bay where the *Swordfish* was stranded there chanced to be a lifeboat. Most of her noble crew were, at the time the vessel struck, in chapel, probably engaged in singing the hymns of the great John Wesley, or listening to the preaching of the "old, old story" of the salvation of souls through faith in Jesus Christ. But there were bodies to be saved that day as well as souls, and the stout arms of the lifeboat crew were needed.

The cry was quickly raised, "A wreck in the bay!" The shout that naturally followed was, "The lifeboat!" A stalwart Cornish gentleman sprang from his pew to serve his Master in another field. He was the Honorary Local Secretary of the Lifeboat Institution — a man brimful of physical energy, and with courage and heart for every good work. No time was lost. Six powerful horses were procured so quickly that it seemed as if they had started ready harnessed into being. Willing hands dragged the lifeboat, mounted on its carriage, from its shed, the horses were attached, and a loud cheer arose as the huge craft was whirled along the road towards the bay. The scene of the wreck was a mile distant, and a large town had to be traversed on the way thither. Hundreds of worshippers were on the streets, returning home, with chastened thoughts and feelings perchance, from church and chapel. There was excitement, however, in their looks, for the echo of that cry, "The lifeboat!" had reached the ears of many, and eager inquiries were being made. Presently the lifeboat itself, with all its peculiar gear, came thundering through the town, rudely dispelling, for a few moments, the solemnity of the Sabbath day. Hundreds of men, women, and children followed in its train, and hundreds more joined at every turn of the main thoroughfare.

"A wreck in the bay!" "Crew in the rigging!" "Mainmast gone!" "She can't hold long together in such a sea!" "We'll be in time yet!" "Hurrah!"

Such were some of the exclamations heard on all sides as the rescuers dashed along, and the excited multitude irresistibly followed. Even females ventured to join the throng, and, holding shawls tightly round their heads and shoulders, went down on the exposed sands and faced the pelting storm.

In less than half an hour after the alarm was given, the lifeboat swept down to the beach, the horses, obedient to the rein, flew round, the boat's bow was presented to the sea, and the carriage thrust as far into the surf as was possible. Then hundreds of willing hands seized the launching ropes, and the boat, with her crew already seated, and the oars out, sprang from her carriage into the hissing flood.

A tremendous billow met her. "Steady lads, give way!" cried the coxswain, on whose steering everything depended at the first plunge. The short oars cracked as the men strained every muscle, and shot the boat, not over, but right through the falling deluge. Of course it was filled, but the discharging tubes freed it in a few seconds, and the cheers of the spectators had scarce burst forth when she rushed out to meet the succeeding breaker. There was another breathless moment, when hundreds of men, eager to vent their surcharged breast in another cheer, could only gaze and gasp – then a roar, a world of falling foam, and the lifeboat was submerged. But the gallant coxswain met the shock straight as an arrow, cleft the billow, and leaped onward – irresistibly onward – over, through, and in the teeth of raging wind and waves, until they were fairly out and dancing on the chaotic ocean.

But, just before this took place, the captain of the *Swordfish*, ignorant of the fact that the lifeboat was hastening to the rescue, unfortunately took a fatal step. Believing that no boat would venture to put off in such a gale, he ordered the ship's launch to be lowered. This was done, but it was immediately upset and stove against the side. Then the jollyboat was lowered, and nine men and the captain got into it. The old Indian officer, with his daughter and all the women and children, were also, with great difficulty, put on board of it.

Captain Phelps was cool and self-possessed in that hour of danger. He steered the boat with consummate skill, and succeeded in keeping her afloat for some time. On she rushed, as if driven by an irresistible impulse, amid the cheers of the crowd, and the prayers of many that she might safely reach the land. The brave fellows who manned her struggled hard and well, but in vain. When the boat was little more three hundred yards from the shore an immense breaker overtook her.

"She'll be swamped!" "She's gone!" "God save her!" and similar cries burst from those on shore. Next moment the wave had the boat in its powerful grasp, tossed her on its crest, whirled her round, and turned her keel up, leaving her freight of human beings struggling in the sea.

Oh! it was a terrible thing for the thousands on land to stand so close to those drowning men and women without the power of stretching out a hand to save! No one could get near them, although they were so near. They were tossed like straws on the raging surf. Now hurled on the crest of a wave, now sucked into the hollow beneath, and overwhelmed again and again. The frail ones of the hapless crew soon perished. The strong men struggled on with desperate energy to reach the shore. Three of them seized the keel of the boat, but three times were they driven from their hold by the force of the seas. Two or three caught at the floating oars, but most of them were soon carried away by the under-current. The captain, however, with five or six of the men, still struggled powerfully for life, and succeeded in swimming close to the beach.

Up to this point there was one of the spectators who had stood behind the shelter of a bush, surveying, with sorrowful countenance, the tragic scene. He was a short, but fine-looking and very athletic man — a champion Cornish wrestler, named William Jeff. He was a first-rate boatman, and a bold swimmer. Fortunately he also possessed a generous, daring heart. When this man saw Captain Phelps near the shore, he sprang forward, dashed into the surf, at the imminent risk of his life, and caught the captain by the hair. The retreating water well-nigh swept the brave rescuer away, but other men of the town, fearless like himself, leaped forward, joined hands, caught hold of Jeff, and hauled him safe ashore along with the captain, who was carried away in a state of insensibility. Again and again, at the risk of his life, did the champion wrestler wrestle with the waves and conquer them! Aided by his daring comrades he dragged three others from the jaws of death. Of those who entered the jolly-boat of the *Swordfish*, only five reached the land. These were all sailors, and one of them, Captain Phelps, was so much exhausted by his exertions that, notwithstanding all that cordials, rubbing, and medical skill could effect, he sank in a few minutes, and died.

But while this was occurring on the beach, another scene of disaster was taking place at the wreck. The lifeboat, after a severe pull of more than an hour, reached the vessel. As she was passing under her stern a great sea struck the boat and immediately capsized her. All on board were at once thrown out. The boat was, however, one of those self-righting crafts, which had just at that time been introduced. She immediately righted, emptied herself, and the crew climbed into her by means of the life-lines festooned round her sides; but the brave coxswain was jammed under her by some wreck, and nearly lost his life — having to dive three or four times before he could extricate himself. When at last dragged into the boat by his comrades he was apparently dead. It was then discovered that the man who had pulled the stroke oar had been swept overboard and carried away. His companions believed him to be lost, but he had on one of the cork life-belts of the Lifeboat Institution, and was by it floated to the shore, where a brave fellow swam his horse out through the surf and rescued him.

Meanwhile, the lifeboat men were so much injured and exhausted that they were utterly incapable of making any attempt to rescue those who remained of the crew of the *Swordfish*. It was as much as they could do to guide the boat again towards the shore, steered by the second coxswain, who, although scarcely able to stand, performed his duty with consummate skill.

Nothing of all this could be seen by the thousands on shore, owing to the spray which thickened the atmosphere, and the distance of the wreck. But when the lifeboat came in sight they soon perceived that something was wrong, and when she drew near they rushed to meet her. Dismay filled every breast when they saw the coxswain carried out apparently dead, with a stream of blood trickling from a wound in his temple, and learned from the worn-out and disabled crew that no rescue had been effected. Immediately the local secretary before mentioned, who had been all this time caring for those already rescued, and preparing for those expected, called for a volunteer crew, and the second coxswain at once shouted, "I'll go again, sir!" This man's bravery produced a wonderful moral effect. He was not permitted to go, being already too much exhausted, but his example caused volunteers to come forward promptly. Among them were men of the coastguard, a body to which the country is deeply indebted for annually saving many lives. Several gentlemen of the town also volunteered. With the new crew, and the chief officer of the coastguard at the helm, the noble boat was launched a second time.

The struggle which followed was tremendous, for they had to pull direct to windward in the teeth of wind and sea. Sometimes the boat would rise almost perpendicularly to the waves, and the spectators gazed with bated breath, fearing that she must turn over; then she would gain a yard or two, and again be checked. Thus, inch by inch, they advanced until the wreck was reached, and the sailors were successfully taken off. But this was not accomplished without damage to the rescuers, one of whom had three ribs broken, while others were more or less injured.

Soon the boat was seen making once more for the beach. On she came on the wings of the wind. As she drew near, the people crowded towards her as far as the angry sea would permit.

"How many saved?" was the anxious question.

As the boat rushed forward, high on the crest of a tumultuous billow, the bowman stood up and shouted, "Nine saved!" and in another moment, amid the ringing cheers of the vast multitude, the lifeboat leaped upon the sand with the rescued men!

"Nine saved!" A pleasant piece of news that to be read next day in the papers by those who contributed to place that lifeboat on the coast; for nine souls saved implies many more souls gladdened and filled with unutterable gratitude to Almighty God.

But "Twenty lost!" A dismal piece of news this to those at whose door the murders will lie till the day of doom. Even John Webster, Esq., grew pale when he heard of it, and his hard heart beat harder than usual against his iron ribs as he sat in the habitation of his soul and gazed at his deceased wife's father over the chimney-piece, until he almost thought the canvas image frowned upon him.

There was more, however, behind these twenty lost lives than Mr. Webster dreamed of. The links in the chains of Providence are curiously intermingled, and it is impossible to say, when one of them gives way, which, or how many, will fall along with it, as the next chapter will show.

CHAPTER V.

Things become shaky, so does Mr. Webster, and the Results are an Illness and a Voyage.

The old Indian officer who was drowned, as we have seen, in the wreck of the *Swordfish*, was in no way connected with Mr. John Webster. In fact, the latter gentleman read his name in the list of those lost with feelings of comparative indifference. He was "very sorry indeed," as he himself expressed it, that so many human beings had been swept off the stage of time by that "unfortunate wreck," but it did not add to his sorrow that an old gentleman, whom he had never seen or heard of before, was numbered with the drowned. Had he foreseen the influence that the death of that old officer was to have on his own fortunes, he might have looked a little more anxiously at the announcement of it. But Colonel Green — that was his name — was nothing to John Webster. What mattered his death or life to him? He was, no doubt, a rich old fellow, who had lived in the East Indies when things were conducted in a rather loose style, and when unscrupulous men in power had opportunities of feathering their nests well; but even although that was true it mattered not, for all Colonel Green's fortune, if thrown into the pile or taken from it, would scarcely have made an appreciable difference in the wealth of the great firm of Webster and Co. Not that "Co." had anything to do with it, for there was no Co. There had been one once, but he had long ago passed into the realms where gold has no value.

There was, however, a very large and important firm in Liverpool which was deeply interested in the life of Colonel Green, for he had long been a sleeping partner of the firm, and had, during a course of years, become so deeply indebted to it that the other partners were beginning to feel uneasy about him. Messrs. Wentworth and Hodge would have given a good deal to have got rid of their sleeping partner, but Colonel Green cared not a straw for Wentworth, nor a fig for Hodge, so he went on in his own way until the *Swordfish* was wrecked, when he went the way of all flesh, and Wentworth and Hodge discovered that, whatever riches he, Colonel Green, might at one time have possessed, he left nothing behind him except a number of heavy debts.

This was serious, because the firm had been rather infirm for some years past, and the consequences of the colonel's death were, that it became still more shaky, and finally came down. Now, it is a well understood fact that men cannot fall alone. You cannot remove a small prop from a large old tree without running the risk of causing the old tree to fall and carry a few of the neighbouring trees, with a host of branches, creeping plants, and parasites, along with it. Especially is this the case in the mercantile world. The death of Colonel Green was a calamity only to a few tradesmen, but the fall of Wentworth and Co. was a much more serious matter, because that firm was an important prop to the much greater firm of Dalgetty and Son, which immediately shook in its shoes, and also went down, spreading ruin and consternation in the city. Now, it happened that Dalgetty and Son had extensive dealings with Webster and Co., and their fall involved the latter so deeply, that, despite their great wealth, their idolatrous head was compelled to puzzle his brain considerably in order to see his way out of his difficulties.

But the more he looked, the less he saw of a favourable nature. Some of his evil practices also had of late begun to shed their legitimate fruit on John Webster, and to teach him something of the meaning of those words, "Be sure your sins shall find you out." This complicated matters considerably. He consulted his cash-books, bank-books, bill-books, sales-books, order-books, ledgers, etc. etc., again and again, for hours at a time, without arriving at any satisfactory result. He went to his diminutive office early in the morning, and sat there late at night; and did not, by so doing, improve his finances a whit, although he succeeded in materially injuring his health. He worried the life of poor meek Grinder to such an extent that that unfortunate man went home one night and told his wife he meant to commit suicide, begged her to go out and purchase a quart of laudanum for that purpose at the fishmonger's, and was not finally induced to give up, or at least to delay, his rash purpose, until he had swallowed a tumbler of mulled port wine and gone to sleep with a bottle of hot water at his feet! In short, Mr. Webster did all that it was possible for a man to do in order to retrieve his fortunes — all except pray, and commit his affairs into the hands of his Maker; *that* he held to be utterly ridiculous. To make use of God's winds, and waves, and natural laws, and the physical and mental powers which had been given him, for the furtherance of his designs, was quite natural, he said; but to make use of God's word and His promises — tut! tut! he said, that was foolishness.

However that may be, the end was, that Webster and Co. became very shaky. They did not, indeed, go into the *Gazette*, but they got into very deep water; and the principal, ere long, having overwrought all his powers, was stricken with a raging fever.

It was then that John Webster found his god to be anything but a comforter, for it sat upon him like a nightmare; and poor Annie, who, assisted by Mrs. Niven, was his constant and devoted nurse, was horrified by the terrible forms in which the golden idol assailed him. That fever became to him the philosopher's stone. Everything was transmuted by it into gold. The counting of guineas was the poor man's sole occupation from morning till night, and the numbers to which he attained were sometimes quite bewildering; but he invariably lost the thread at a certain point, and, with a weary sigh, began over again at the beginning. The bed curtains became golden tissue, the quilt golden filigree, the posts golden masts and yards and bowsprits, which now receded from him to immeasurable distance, and anon advanced, until he cried out and put up his hands to shield his face from harm; but, whether they advanced or retired, they invariably ended by being wrecked, and he was left in the raging sea surrounded by drowning men, with whom he grappled and fought like a demon, insomuch that it was found necessary at one time to have a strong man in an adjoining room, to be ready to come in when summoned, and hold him down. Gold, gold, gold was the subject of his thoughts — the theme of his ravings — at that time. He must have read, at some period of his life, and been much impressed by, Hood's celebrated poem on that subject, for he was constantly quoting scraps of it.

"Why don't you help me?" he would cry at times, turning fiercely to his daughter. "How can I remember it if I am not helped? I have counted it all up — one, two, three, on to millions, and billions, and trillions of gold, gold, gold, hammered and rolled, bought and sold, scattered and doled — there, I've lost it again! You are constantly setting me wrong. All the things about me are gold, and the very food you gave me yesterday was gold. Oh! how sick I am of this gold! Why don't you take it away from me?"

And then he would fall into some other train of thought, in which his god, as before, would take the reins and drive him on, ever in the same direction.

At last the crisis of the disease came and passed, and John Webster began slowly to recover. And it was now that he formed a somewhat true estimate of the marketable value of his daughter Annie, inasmuch as he came at length to the conclusion that she was priceless, and that he would not agree to sell her for any sum that could be named!

During this period of convalescence, Annie's patience, gentleness, and powers of endurance were severely tried, and not found wanting. The result was that the conscience of the invalid began to awake and smite him; then his heart began to melt, and, ere long, became knit to that of his child, while she sought to relieve his pains and cheer his spirits she chatted, played, sang, and read to him. Among other books she read the Bible. At first Mr. Webster objected to this, on the ground that he did not care for it; but, seeing that Annie was much pained by his refusal, he consented to permit her to read a few verses to him daily. He always listened to them with his eyes shut, but never by look or comment gave the least sign that they made any impression on him.

During the whole period of Mr. Webster's illness and convalescence, Captain Harry Boyns found it convenient to have much business to transact in Liverpool, and he was extremely regular in his calls to inquire after the health of his late employer. This was very kind of him, considering the way in which he had been treated! Sometimes on these visits he saw Annie, sometimes he saw Mrs. Niven — according as the one or other chanced to be on duty at the time; but, although he was never permitted to do more than exchange a few sentences with either of them, the most careless observer could have told, on each occasion, which he had seen, for he always left the door with a lengthened face and slow step when he had seen Mrs. Niven: but ran down the steps with a flushed countenance and sparkling eyes when he had met with Annie!

At last Mr. Webster was so much restored that his doctor

gave him leave to pay a short visit to his counting-room in the city.

How strangely Mr. Webster felt, after his long absence, when he entered once more the temple of his god, and sat down in his old chair. Everything looked so familiar, yet so strange! There were, indeed, the old objects, but not the old arrangements, for advantage had been taken of his absence to have the office "thoroughly cleaned!" There was the same air of quiet, too, and seclusion; but the smells were not so musty as they used to be, and there was something terribly unbusinesslike in the locked desk and the shut books and the utter absence of papers. The portrait of his deceased wife's father was there, however, as grim, silent, and steadfast in its gaze as ever, so Mr. Webster smiled, nodded to it, and rang a hand-bell for his confidential clerk, who entered instantly, having been stationed at the back of the door for full ten minutes in expectation of the summons.

"Good morning, Mr. Grinder. I have been ill, you see. Glad to get back, however. How has business been going on in my absence? The doctor forbade my making any inquiries while I was ill, so that I have been rather anxious."

"Yes, sir, I am aware — I—in fact I was anxious to see you several times on business, but could not gain admittance."

"H'm! not going on so well as might be desired, I suppose," said Mr. Webster.

"Well, not quite; in short, I might even say things are much worse than they were before you took ill, sir; but if a confidential agent were sent to Jamaica to — to—that is, if Messrs. Bright and Early were seen by yourself, sir, and some arrangement made, we might — might — go on for some time longer, and if trade revives, I think — "

"So bad as that!" exclaimed Mr. Webster, musing. "Well, well, Grinder, we must do our best to pull through. Are any of our vessels getting ready for sea just now?"

"Yes, sir, the *Ocean Queen* sails for Jamaica about the end of this month."

"Very well, Grinder, I will go in her. She is one of our best ships, I think. The doctor said something about a short voyage to recruit me, so that's settled. Bring me writing materials, and send a statement of affairs home to me to-night. I have not yet strength to go into details here."

Grinder brought the writing materials and retired. His employer wrote several letters; among them one to the doctor, apprising him of his intention to go to Jamaica, and another to the captain of the *Ocean Queen*, giving him the same information, and directing him to fit up the two best berths in the cabin for the reception of himself and his daughter, with a berth for an old female servant.

Three weeks thereafter he went on board with Annie and Mrs. Niven, and the *Ocean Queen*, spreading her sails, was soon far out upon the broad bosom of the restless Atlantic.

CHAPTER VI.

Describes the Presentation of a New Lifeboat to Covelly,
and treats of The Royal National Lifeboat Institution.

We must now change the scene, and beg our readers to accompany us once more to Covelly, where, not long after the events narrated in the last chapter, an interesting ceremony was performed, which called out the inhabitants in vast numbers. This was the presentation of a new lifeboat to the town, and the rewarding of several men who had recently been instrumental in saving life in circumstances of peculiar danger.

The weather was propitious. A bright sun and a calm sea rejoiced the eyes of the hundreds who had turned out to witness the launch. The old boat, which had saved our heroine years before, and had rescued many more since that day from the angry sea, was worn out, and had to be replaced by one of the magnificent new boats built on the self-righting principle, which had but recently been adopted by the Lifeboat Institution. A lady of the neighbourhood, whose only daughter had been saved by the old boat some time before, had presented the purchase-money of the new one (£400) to the Institution; and, with the promptitude which characterises all the movements of that Society, a fine self-righting lifeboat, with all the latest improvements, had been sent at once to the port.

High on her carriage, in the centre of the town, the new lifeboat stood — gay and brilliant in her blue and white paint, the crew with their cork lifebelts on, and a brass band in front, ready to herald her progress to the shore. The mayor of the town, with all the principal men, headed the procession, and a vast concourse of people followed. At the shore the boat was named the *Rescue* by the young lady whose life had been saved by the old one, and amid the acclamations of the vast multitude, the noble craft was shot off her carriage into the calm sea, where she was rowed about for a considerable time, and very critically examined by her crew; for, although the whole affair was holiday-work to most of those who looked on, the character of the new boat was a matter of serious import to those who manned her, and who might be called on to risk their lives in her every time their shores should be lashed by a stormy sea.

Our hero, Harry Boyns, held the steering oar. He had been appointed by the parent Institution to the position of "Local Secretary of the Covelly Lifeboat Branch," and, of course, was anxious to know the qualities of his vessel.

Harry, we may remark in passing, having lost his situation, and finding that his mother's health was failing, had made up his mind to stay on shore for a year or two, and seek employment in his native town. Being a well-educated man, he obtained this in the office of a mercantile house, one of the partners of which was related to his mother.

The rowing powers of the new boat were soon tested. Then Harry steered to the pier, where a tackle had been prepared for the purpose of upsetting her. This was an interesting point in the proceedings, because few there had seen a self-righting boat, and, as usual, there was a large sprinkling in the crowd of that class of human beings who maintain the plausible, but false, doctrine, that "seeing is believing!"

Considerable difficulty was experienced in getting the boat to overturn. The operation was slowly accomplished; and all through there appeared to be an unwillingness on the part of the boat to upset! — a symptom which gave much satisfaction to her future crew, who stood ready on her gunwale to leap away from her. At last she was raised completely on one side, then she balanced for a moment, and fell forward, keel up, with a tremendous splash, while the men, not a moment too soon, sprang into the sea, and a wild cheer, mingled with laughter, arose from the spectators.

If the upsetting was slow and difficult, the self-righting was magically quick and easy. The boat went right round, and, almost before one could realise what had occurred, she was again on an even keel. Of course she was nearly full of water at the moment of rising; but, in a few seconds, the discharging holes in her bottom had cleared the water completely away. The whole operation of self-righting and self-emptying, from first to last, occupied only *seventeen seconds*! If there was laughter mingled with the shouts when she overturned and threw her crew into the sea, there was nothing but deep-toned enthusiasm in the prolonged cheer which hailed her on righting, for then it was fully realised, especially by seafaring men, what genuine and valuable qualities the boat possessed, and the cheers became doubly enthusiastic when the crew, grasping the lifelines which were festooned round her sides, clambered on board again, and were reseated at the oars in less than two minutes thereafter.

This done, the boat was hauled up on her carriage, and conveyed to the house near the beach which had been prepared for her reception, there to wait, in constant readiness, until the storm should call her forth to display her peculiar qualities in actual service.

But another, and, if possible, a still more interesting ceremony remained to be performed. This was the presentation of the gold and silver medals of the Institution to several men of the town, who, in a recent storm, had rendered signal service in the saving of human life.

The zealous and indefatigable secretary of the Institution had himself come down from London to present these.

The presentation took place in the new town hall, a large building capable of containing upwards of a thousand people, which, on the occasion, was filled to overflowing.

The mayor presided, of course, and opened proceedings, as many chairmen do, by taking the wind out of the sails of the principal speaker! That is to say, he touched uninterestingly on each topic that was likely to engage the attention of the meeting, and stated many facts and figures in a loose and careless way, which every one knew the secretary would, as a matter of course, afterwards state much better and more correctly than himself. But the mayor was a respected, well-meaning man, and, although his speech was listened to with manifest impatience, his sitting down was hailed with rapturous applause.

At this point — the mayor having in his excitement forgotten to call upon the secretary to speak — a stout man on the platform took advantage of the oversight and started to his feet, calling from a disgusted auditor the expression, "Oh, there's that bore Dowler!" It was indeed that same Joseph who had, on a memorable occasion long past, signed himself the "humble" friend of Mr. Webster. Before a word could escape his lips, however, he was greeted with a storm of yells and obliged to sit down. But he did so under protest, and remained watchful for another favourable opportunity of breaking in. Dowler never knew when he was "out of order;" he never felt or believed himself to be "out of order!" In fact, he did not know what "out of order" meant *when applied to himself.* He was morally a rhinoceros. He could not be shamed by disapprobation; could not be cowed by abuse; never was put out by noise — although he frequently was by the police; nor put down by reason — though he sometimes was by force; spoke everywhere, on all subjects, against the opinions (apparently) of everybody; and lived a life of perpetual public martyrdom and protest.

Silence having been obtained, the secretary of the Lifeboat Institution rose, and, after a few complimentary remarks on the enthusiasm in the good cause shown by the town, and especially by the lady who had presented the boat, he called Captain Harry Boyns to the platform, and presented him with the gold medal of the Institution in an able speech, wherein he related the special act of gallantry for which it was awarded — telling how that, during a terrible gale, on a dark night in December, the gallant young captain, happening to walk homewards along the cliffs, observed a vessel on the rocks, not twenty yards from the land, with the green seas making clean breaches over her; and how that — knowing the tide was rising, and that before he could run to the town, three miles distant, for assistance, the vessel would certainly be dashed to pieces — he plunged into the surf, at the imminent risk of his life, swam to the vessel, and returned to the shore with a rope, by which means a hawser was fixed to the cliffs, and thirty-nine lives were rescued from the sea!

Well did every one present know the minute details of the heroic deed referred to, but they were glad to hear the praises of their townsman re-echoed by one who thoroughly understood the merits of the case, and whose comments thereon brought out more clearly to the minds of many the extent of the danger which the gallant captain had run, so that, when Harry stepped forward to receive the medal, he was greeted with the most enthusiastic cheers. Thereafter, the secretary presented silver medals to two fishermen of the Cove, namely, Old Jacobs and Robert Gaston, both of whom had displayed unusual daring at the rescue of the young lady who was the donor of the lifeboat. He then touched on the value of lifeboats in general, and gave an interesting account of the origin of the Society which he represented; but as this subject deserves somewhat special treatment, we shall turn aside from the thread of our tale for a little, to regard the Work and the Boats of the Royal National Lifeboat Institution, assuring our reader that the subject is well worthy the earnest consideration of all men.

The first lifeboat ever launched upon the stormy sea was planned and built by a London coach-builder, named Lionel Lukin, who took out a patent for it in November 1785, and launched it at Bamborough, where it was the means of saving many lives the first year. Although Lukin thus demonstrated the possibility of lives being saved by a boat which could live under circumstances that would have proved fatal to ordinary boats, he was doomed to disappointment. The Prince of Wales (George IV.) did indeed befriend him, but the Lords of Admiralty were deaf, and the public were indifferent. Lukin went to his grave unrewarded by man, but stamped with a nobility which can neither be gifted nor inherited, but only won – the nobility which attaches to the character of "national benefactor."

The public were aroused from their apathy in 1789 by the wreck of the *Adventure* of Newcastle, the crew of which perished in the presence of thousands, who could do nothing to save them. Models of lifeboats were solicited, and premiums offered for the best. Among those who responded, William Wouldhave, a painter, and Henry Greathead, a boat-builder of South Shields, stood pre-eminent. The latter afterwards became a noted builder and improver of lifeboats, and was well and deservedly rewarded for his labours. In 1803 Greathead had built thirty-one boats – eighteen for England, five for Scotland, and eight for other countries. This was, so far, well, but it was a wretchedly inadequate provision for the necessities of the case. It was not until 1822 that a great champion of the lifeboat cause stood forth in the person of

Sir William Hillary, Bart.

Sir William, besides being a philanthropist, was a hero! He not only devised liberal things and carried them into execution, but he personally shared in the danger of rescuing life from the sea. He dwelt on the shores of the Isle of Man, where he established a Sailors' Home at Douglas. He frequently embarked in the boats that went off to rescue lives from the wrecks that were constantly occurring on the island. Once he had his ribs broken in this service, and was frequently in imminent danger of being drowned. During his career he personally assisted in the saving of 305 human lives! He was the means of stirring up public men, and the nation generally, to a higher sense of their duty towards those who, professionally and otherwise, risk their lives upon the sea; and eventually, in conjunction with two Members of Parliament — Mr. Thomas Wilson and Mr. George Herbert — was the founder of *"The Royal National Institution for the Preservation of Life from Shipwreck."* This Institution — now named *The Royal National Lifeboat Institution* — was founded on the 24th of March 1824, and has gone on progressively, doing its noble work of creating and maintaining a lifeboat fleet, rescuing the shipwrecked, and rewarding the rescuers, from that day to this. When life does not require to be saved, and when opportunity offers, the Society allows its boats to save *property*, of which we shall have something more to say presently.

At the founding of the Institution in 1824, the Archbishop of Canterbury of the day filled the chair; the great Wilberforce, Lord John Russell, and other magnates, were present; the Dukes of Kent, Sussex, and other members of the Royal family, became vice-patrons; the Duke of Northumberland its vice-president, and George IV. its patron. In 1850 the much-lamented Prince Albert — whose life was a continual going about doing good — became its vice-patron, and Her Majesty the Queen became, and still continues, a warm supporter and an annual contributor.

Now, this is a splendid array of names and titles; but it ought ever to be borne in remembrance that the Institution is dependent for its continued existence on the public — on you and me, good reader — for it is supported almost entirely by voluntary contributions. That it will always find warm hearts to pray for it, and open hands to give, as long as its boats continue, year by year, to pluck men, women, and children from the jaws of death, and give them back to gladdened hearts on shore, is made very apparent from the records published quarterly in *The Lifeboat Journal* of the Society, a work full of interesting information. Therein we find that the most exalted contributor is Queen Victoria — the lowliest, a sailor's orphan child!

Here are a few of the gifts to the Institution selected very much at random: — One gentleman leaves it a legacy of £10,000. Some time ago a sum of £5000 was sent anonymously by "a friend." There comes £100 as a second donation from a sailor's daughter, and £50 from a British admiral. Five shillings are sent as "the savings of a child"; 1s. 6d. from another little child, in postage-stamps; £15 from "three fellow-servants"; £10 from "a shipwrecked pilot," and 10s. 6d. from "an old salt." Indeed, we can speak from personal experience on this subject, because, among others, we received a letter, one day, in a cramped and peculiar hand, which we perused with deep interest, for it had been written by a *blind* youth, whose eyes, nevertheless, had been thoroughly opened to see the great importance of the lifeboat cause, for he had collected £100 for the Institution! On another occasion, at the close of a lecture on the subject, an old woman, who appeared to be among the poorest of the classes who inhabit the old town of Edinburgh, came to us and said, "Hae, there's tippence for the lifeboat!"

It cannot be doubted that these sums, and many, many

others that are presented annually, are the result of moral influences which elevate the soul, and which are indirectly caused by the lifeboat service. We therefore hold that the Institution ought to be regarded as a prolific cause of moral good to the nation. And, while we are on this subject, it may be observed that our lifeboat influence for good on other nations is very considerable. In proof of this we cite the following facts: — Finland sends £50 to our Institution to testify its appreciation of the good done by us to its sailors and shipping. The late President Lincoln of the United States, while involved in all the anxieties of the great civil war, found time to send £100 to our Lifeboat Institution, in acknowledgement of the services rendered to American ships in distress. Russia and Holland send naval men to inspect our lifeboat management. France, in generous emulation of ourselves, starts a Lifeboat Institution of its own; and last, but not least, it has been said, that "foreigners know when they are wrecked on the shores of Britain by the persevering and noble efforts that are made to save their lives!"

But there are some minds which do not attach much value to moral influence, and to which material benefit is an all-powerful argument. Well, then, to these we would address ourselves, but, in passing, would remark that moral influence goes far to secure for us material advantage. It is just because so many hundreds of human living souls are annually preserved to us that men turn with glowing gratitude to the rescuers and to the Institution which organises and utilises the latent philanthropy and pluck of our coast heroes. On an average, 800 lives are saved *every year*, while, despite our utmost efforts, 600 are lost. Those who know anything about our navy, and our want of British seamen to man our ships, cannot fail to see that the saving of so many valuable lives is a positive material benefit to the nation. But to descend to the lowest point, we maintain that the value of the lifeboats to the nation, in the mere matter of saving property, is almost incredible. In regard to these things, it is possible to speak definitely.

For instance, during stormy weather, it frequently happens that vessels show signals of distress, either because they are so badly strained as to be in a sinking condition, or so damaged that they are unmanageable, or the crews have become so exhausted as to be no longer capable of working for their own preservation. In such cases, the lifeboat puts off with the intention, *in the first instance*, of saving *life*. It reaches the vessel in distress; the boat's crew spring on board and find, perhaps, that there is some hope of saving the ship. Knowing the locality well, they steer her clear of rocks and shoals. Being fresh and vigorous, they work the pumps with a will, manage to keep her afloat, and finally steer her into port, thus saving ship and cargo as well as crew.

Now, let it be observed that what we have here supposed is not imaginary — it is not even of rare occurrence. It happens every year. Last year thirty-eight ships were thus saved by lifeboats. The year before, twenty-eight were saved. The year before that, seventeen. Before that, twenty-one. As surely and regularly as the year comes round, so surely and regularly are ships and property thus saved *to the nation*.

It cannot be too well understood that a wrecked ship is not only an individual, but a national loss. Insurance protects the individual, but insurance cannot, in the nature of things, protect the nation. If you drop a thousand sovereigns in the street, that is a loss to *you*, but not to the *nation*. Some lucky individual will find the money and circulate it. But if you drop it in the sea, it is lost, not only to you, but to the nation to which you belong — ay, lost to the world itself for ever! If a lifeboat, therefore, saves a ship worth £1000 from destruction, it literally presents that sum as a free gift to the nation. We say a free gift, because the lifeboats are supported for the purpose of saving life, not property.

A few remarks on the value of loaded ships will throw additional light on this subject, and make more apparent the value of the Lifeboat Institution. Take, first, the case of a ship which was actually saved by a lifeboat. She was a large Spanish ship, which grounded on a bank off the south coast of Ireland. The captain and crew forsook her, and escaped to shore in their boats, but one man was inadvertently left on board. Soon after, the wind moderated and shifted, the ship slipped off the bank into deep water, and drifted to the northward. The crew of the *Cahore* lifeboat were on the look-out, observed the vessel passing, launched their boat, and after a long pull against wind and sea, boarded the vessel, and rescued the Spanish sailor. But they did more. Finding seven feet of water in the hold, they rigged the pumps, trimmed the sails, carried the ship into port, and handed her over to an agent for the owners. This vessel and cargo were valued at £20,000, and we think we are justified in saying that England, through the instrumentality of her Lifeboat Institution, presented that handsome sum to Spain upon that occasion!

But many ships are much more costly than that was. Some time ago a ship named the *Golden Age* was lost upon our shores; it was valued at £200,000. If that single ship had been one of the thirty-eight saved last year (and it might have been), the sum thus saved to the nation would have been more than sufficient to buy up all the lifeboats in the kingdom twice over! But that ship was not amongst the saved. It was lost. So was the *Ontario* of Liverpool, which was wrecked in October 1864, and valued at £100,000. Also the *Assaye*, wrecked on the Irish coast, and valued at £200,000. Here are £500,000 lost for ever by the wreck of these three ships alone in one year! Do you know, reader, what such sums represent? Are you aware that the value of the *Ontario* alone is equal to the income for one year of the London Missionary

Society, wherewith it supports its institutions at home and abroad, and spreads the blessed knowledge of gospel truth over a vast portion of the globe?

But we have only spoken of three ships — no doubt three of the largest size — yet only three of the lost. Couple the above figures with the fact that the number of ships lost, or seriously damaged, *every year*, on the shores of the United Kingdom is above *two thousand*, and you will have some idea of one of the reasons why taxation is so heavy; and if you couple them with the other fact, that, from twenty to thirty ships, great and small, are saved by lifeboats every year, you will perceive that, whatever amount may be given to the Lifeboat Institution, it gives back to the nation *far more* than it receives in *material wealth*, not to mention human lives at all.

Its receipts in 1868 from all sources were £31,668, and its expenditure £31,585. The lives saved by its own boats last year were 603, in addition to which other 259 were saved by shore boats, for which the Institution rewarded the crews with thirteen medals, and money to the extent of above £6573, for all services.

The Lifeboat Institution has a little sister, whom it would be unjust, as well as ungracious, not to introduce in passing, namely, the **Shipwrecked Mariners' Society**. They do their blessed work hand in hand. Their relative position may be simply stated thus: — The Lifeboat Institution saves life. Having dragged the shipwrecked sailor from the sea, its duty is done. It hands him over to the agent of the Shipwrecked Mariners' Society, who takes him by the hand, sees him housed, warmed, clad and fed, and sends him home rejoicing, free of expense, and with a little cash in his pocket. Formerly, shipwrecked sailors had to beg their way to their homes. At first they were sympathised with and well treated. Thereupon uprose a host of counterfeits. The land was overrun by shipwrecked-mariner-beggars, and as people of the interior knew not which was which, poor shipwrecked Jack often suffered because of these vile impostors. But now there is not a port in the kingdom without its agent of the Society. Jack has, therefore, no need to beg his way. "The world" knows this; the deceiver knows it too, therefore his occupation is gone! Apart from its benignant work, the mere fact that the "little sister" has swept such vagrants off the land entitles her to a strong claim on our gratitude. She, also, is supported by voluntary contributions.

Turning now to another branch of our subject, let us regard for a little the boats of the Lifeboat Institution.

"What is a lifeboat? Wherein does it differ from other boats?" are questions sometimes put. Let us attempt a brief reply.

A lifeboat — that is to say, the present lifeboat — differs from all other boats in four particulars: — 1. It is *almost* indestructible. 2. It is insubmergible. 3. It is self-righting. 4. It is self-emptying. In other words, it can hardly be destroyed; it cannot be sunk; it rights itself if upset; it empties itself if filled. Let us illustrate these points in succession. Here is evidence on the first point.

On a terrible night in 1857 a Portuguese brig struck on the Goodwin Sands. The noble, and now famous, Ramsgate lifeboat was at once towed out when the signal-rocket from the lightship was seen, indicating "a wreck on the sands." A terrific battle with the winds and waves ensued. At length the boat was cast off to windward of the sands, and bore down on the brig through the shoal water, which tossed her like a cork on its raging surface. They reached the brig and lay by her for some time in the hope of getting her off, but failed. The storm increased, the vessel began to break up, so her crew were taken into the boat, which — having previously cast anchor to windward of the wreck, and eased off the cable until it got under her lee — now tried to pull back to its anchor. Every effort was fruitless, owing to the shifting nature of the sands and the fury of the storm. At last nothing was left for it but to hoist the sail, cut the cable, and make a desperate effort to beat off the sands. In this also they failed; were caught on the crest of a breaking roller, and borne away to leeward. Water and wind in wildest commotion were comparatively small matters to the lifeboat, but want of water was a serious matter. The tide happened to be out. The sands were only partially covered, and over them the breakers swept in a chaotic seething turmoil that is inconceivable by those who have not witnessed it. Every one has seen the ripples on the seashore when the tide is out. On the Goodwins these ripples are great banks, to be measured by yards instead of inches. From one to another of these sand-banks this boat was cast. Each breaker caught her up, hurled her onward a few yards, and let her down with a crash that well-nigh tore every man out of her, leaving her there a few moments, to be caught up again and made sport with by the next billow. The Portuguese sailors, eighteen in number, clung to the thwarts in silent despair, but the crew of the boat did not lose heart. They knew her splendid qualities, and hoped that, if they should only escape being dashed against the portions of wreck which strewed the sands, all might yet be well. Thus, literally fathom by fathom, with a succession of shocks that would have knocked any ordinary boat to pieces, was this magnificent lifeboat driven, during two hours in the dead of night, over two miles of the Goodwin Sands! At last she drove into deep water on the other side; the sails were set, and soon after, through God's mercy, the rescued men were landed safely in Ramsgate Harbour. So, we repeat, the lifeboat is almost indestructible.

That she is insubmergible has been proved by what has already been written, and our space forbids giving further illustration, but a word about the cause of this quality is necessary. Her floating power is due to *air-chambers* fitted round the sides under the seats and in the bow and stern; also to empty space and light wood or cork ballast under her floor. If thrust forcibly deep under water with as many persons in her as could be stowed away, she would, on being released, rise again to the surface like a cork.

The self-righting principle is one of the most important qualities of the lifeboat. However good it may be in other respects, a boat without this quality is a lifeboat only so long as it maintains its proper position on the water. If upset it is no better than any other boat. It is true that, great stability being one of the lifeboat's qualities, such boats are not easily overturned. Nevertheless they sometimes are so, and the results have been on several occasions disastrous. Witness the case of the Liverpool boat, which in January 1865 upset, and the crew of seven men were drowned. Also the Point of Ayr lifeboat, which upset when under sail at a distance from the land, and her crew, thirteen in number, were drowned. Two or three of the poor fellows were seen clinging to the keel for twenty minutes, but no assistance could be rendered. Now, both of these were considered good lifeboats, but they were *not self-righting*. Numerous cases might be cited to prove the inferiority of the non-self-righting boats, but one more will suffice. In February 1858 the Southwold boat — a large sailing boat, esteemed one of the finest in the kingdom, but *not* self-righting — went out for exercise, and was running before a heavy surf with all sail set, when she suddenly ran on the top of a sea, broached-to and upset. The crew in this case being near shore, and having on cork lifebelts, were rescued, but three gentlemen who had gone off in her without lifebelts were drowned. This case, and the last, occurred in broad daylight.

In contrast to these we give an instance of the action of the self-righting lifeboat when overturned. It occurred on a dark stormy night in October 1858. On that night a wreck took place off the coast near Dungeness, three miles from shore. The small lifeboat belonging to that place put off to the rescue. Eight stout men of the coastguard composed her crew. She belonged to the National Lifeboat Institution — all the boats of which are now built on the self-righting principle. The wreck was reached soon after midnight, and found to have been deserted by her crew; the boat therefore returned to the shore. While crossing a deep channel between two shoals she was caught up and struck by three heavy seas in succession. The coxswain lost command of the rudder, and she was carried away before a sea, broached to and upset, throwing the men out of her. Immediately she righted herself, cleared herself of water, and the anchor having fallen out she was brought up by it. The crew, meanwhile, having on life-belts, regained the boat, got into her by means of the lifelines hung round her sides, cut the cable, and returned to the shore in safety!

The means by which the self-righting is accomplished are — two large air-cases, one in the bow, the other in the stern, and a heavy iron keel. These air-cases are rounded on the top and raised so high that a boat, bottom up, resting on them, would be raised almost quite out of the water. Manifestly, to rest on these pivots is an impossibility; the overturned boat *must* fall on its side, in which position the heavy iron keel comes into play and drags the bottom down, thus placing the boat violently and quickly in her proper position. The simple plan here described was invented by the Rev. James Bremner, of Orkney, and exhibited at Leith, near Edinburgh, in the year 1800. Mr. Bremner's aircases were empty casks in the bow and stern, and his ballast was three hundred-weight of iron attached to the keel.

This plan, however, was not made practically useful until upwards of fifty years later, when twenty out of twenty-four men were lost by the upsetting of the *non-self-righting* lifeboat of South

Shields. After the occurrence of that melancholy event, the late Duke of Northumberland — who for many years was one of the warmest supporters and patrons of the Lifeboat Institution — offered a prize of £100 for the best self-righting lifeboat. It was gained by Mr. Beeching, whose boat was afterwards considerably altered and improved by Mr. Peak.

The self-emptying principle is of almost equal importance with the self-righting, for, in every case of putting off to a wreck, a lifeboat is necessarily filled again and again with water — sometimes overwhelmed by tons of it; and a boat full of water, however safe it may be, is necessarily useless. Six large holes in the bottom of the boat effect the discharge of water. There is an airtight floor to the lifeboat, which is so placed that when the boat is fully manned and loaded with passengers it is *a very little above the level of the sea*. On this fact the acting of the principle depends. Between this floor and the bottom of the boat, a space of upwards of a foot in depth, there is some light ballast of cork or wood, and some parts of the space are left empty. The six holes above mentioned are tubes of six inches diameter, which extend from the floor through the bottom of the boat. Now, it is one of nature's laws that water *must* find its level. For instance, take any boat and bore large holes in its bottom, and suppose it to be held up in its *ordinary* floating position, so that it cannot sink, then fill it suddenly quite full of water, it will be found that the water *inside* will run out until it is on a level with the water *outside*. Water poured into a lifeboat will of course act in the same way, but when that which has been poured into it reaches the level of the water outside, *it has also reached the floor*: in other words, there is no more water left to run out.

Such are the principal qualities of the splendid lifeboat now used on our coasts, and of which it may be said that it has almost reached the state of absolute perfection.

The Lifeboat Institution, which has been the means in God's hands of saving so many thousands of human lives, is now in a high state of efficiency and of well-deserved prosperity; both of which conditions are due very largely to the untiring exertions and zeal of its present secretary, Richard Lewis, Esq., of the Inner Temple. Success is not dependent on merit alone. Good though the lifeboat cause unquestionably is, we doubt whether the Institution would have attained its present high position so soon, had it not been guided thereto by the judicious management of its committee – the members of which bestow laborious and gratuitous service on its great and national work – aided by the able and learned secretary and an experienced inspector of lifeboats (Captain J.R. Ward, R.N.) both whose judgement and discretion have often been the themes of deserved praise by the public.

That the claims of the Institution are very strong must be admitted by all who reflect that during upwards of forty years it has been engaged in the grand work of saving human lives. Up to the present date, it has plucked 18,225 human beings from the waves, besides an incalculable amount of valuable property. It is a truly national blessing, and as such deserves the support of every man and woman in the kingdom. (See footnote.)

But, to return from this prolonged yet by no means unnecessary digression, – let us remind the reader that we left him at the meeting in the town-hall of Covelly, of which, however, we will only say further, that it was very enthusiastic and most successful. That the mayor, having been stirred in spirit by the secretary's speech, redeemed himself by giving vent to a truly eloquent oration, and laying on the table a handsome contribution towards the funds of the Society. That many of the people present gladly followed his lead, and that the only interruption to the general harmony was the repeated attempts made by Mr. Joseph Dowler – always out of order – to inflict himself upon the meeting; an infliction which the meeting persistently declined to permit!

Thereafter the new lifeboat was conveyed to its house on the shore, where, however, it had not rested many weeks before it was called into vigorous action.

CHAPTER VII.

The Storm and the Wreck.

Listen, O ye who lie comfortably asleep, secure in your homes, oblivious of danger, when the tempest is roaring overhead! Come, let us together wing our flight to the seashore, and cast a searching glance far and near over the strand.

On a certain Friday morning in the year 18 — , a terrific gale broke over the east coast, and everywhere the lifeboat men went out to watch the raging sea, knowing full well that ere long there would be rough but glorious work for them to do. A tremendous sea ran high on the bar at Tynemouth, and rolled with tremendous force on the Black Middens — rocks that are black indeed, in their history as well as their aspect. A barque was seen making for the Tyne, towed by a steam-tug. A sudden squall struck them; the tug was forced to let the vessel go, and she went on the rocks. A few minutes had barely passed when another vessel was descried, a brig, which made for the harbour, missed it, and was driven on the same fatal rocks a few yards south of the barque. The alarm-gun was fired, and the members of the Tynemouth *Volunteer Life Brigade* were quickly at the scene of disaster. The rocket apparatus was fired, and a line passed over one of the vessels; but other anxious eyes had been on the look-out that night, and soon the salvage boat *William* was launched at North Shields, and the South Shields men launched the Tynemouth lifeboat. The *Constant* lifeboat also put off to the rescue. It was getting dark by that time, so that those on shore could not see the boats after they had engaged in strife with the raging sea. Meanwhile part of the crew of the barque were saved by the rocket apparatus, but those of the brig did not know how to use it, and they would certainly have perished had not the *William* got alongside and rescued them all. While this was going on a third vessel was driven ashore on the Battery Rock. The South Shields lifeboat made towards her, succeeded in getting alongside, and rescued the crew.

A mile west of Folkestone Harbour a brigantine, laden with rum and sugar, went ashore, broadside-on, near Sandgate Castle. The ever-ready coastguardsmen turned out. A Sandgate fisherman first passed a small grapnel on board, then the coastguard sent out a small line with a lifebuoy attached and one by one the crew were all saved — the men of the coastguard with ropes round their waists, standing in the surf as deep as they dared to venture, catching the men who dropped, and holding their heads above water until they were safe. But the gallant coastguardsmen had other work cut out for them that night. Besides saving life, it was their duty to protect property. The cargo was a tempting one to many roughs who had assembled. When the tide receded, these attempted to get on board the wreck and regale themselves. The cutlasses of the coastguard, however, compelled them to respect the rights of private property, and taught them the majesty of the law!

Elsewhere along the coast many vessels were wrecked, and many lives were lost that night, while many more were saved by the gallant lifeboat crews, the details of which, if written, would thrill many a sympathetic breast from John o' Groat's to the Land's End; but passing by these we turn to one particular vessel which staggered in the gale of that night, but which, fortunately for those on board, was still at some distance from the dangerous and dreaded shore.

It was the *Ocean Queen*. Mr. Webster was seated in her cabin, his face very pale, and his hands grasping the arms of the locker tightly to prevent his being hurled to leeward. Annie sat beside him with her arms round his waist. She was alarmed and looked anxious, but evidently possessed more courage than her father. There was some reason for this, however, for she did not know that Mr Webster's fortunes had got into such a desperate case, that for the retrieving of them he depended very much on the successful voyage of the *Ocean Queen*.

"Don't be so cast down, father," said Annie; "I heard the captain say that we shall be in sight of land to-morrow."

"Heaven forbid," said Mr. Webster. "Better to be in mid-ocean than near land on such a night."

Annie was about to reply when the door opened, and the captain looked in. He wore a sou'-wester, and was clad in oilcloth garments from head to foot, which shone like black satin with the dripping spray.

"We're getting on famously," he said in a hearty tone, "the wind has shifted round to the sou'-west, and if it holds — we shall — "

"Sprung a leak, sir!" cried the first mate in a deep excited voice as he looked down the companion.

"What!" exclaimed the captain, rushing upon deck.

"Plank must have started, sir, there's three foot water in — "

His voice was drowned by distance and the roaring of the gale, but Mr. Webster and Annie had heard enough to fill them with alarm.

The *Ocean Queen* had indeed sprung a leak, and so bad was it that when all the pumps available were set a-going, they failed to reduce the depth of water in the hold. Still, by constantly changing hands and making strenuous exertions, they prevented it from increasing rapidly. All that night and next day they wrought with unflagging energy at the pumps. No man on board spared himself. The captain took his spell with the rest. Even Mr. Webster threw off his coat and went to work as if he had been born and bred a coal-heaver. The work, however, was very exhausting, and when land appeared no one seemed to have any heart to welcome it except Annie and her old nurse Mrs. Niven.

Towards evening of the next day the captain came up to Mr. Webster, who was seated on the cabin skylight with his head resting wearily on his hands.

"We cannot make the port of Liverpool, I find," he said. "The pilot says that if we wish to save the ship we must run for the nearest harbour on the coast, which happens, unfortunately, to be the very small one of Covelly."

"Then by all means run for it," said Mr. Webster. "Strange," he muttered to himself, "that fate should lead me there."

The head of the *Ocean Queen* was at once turned towards the shore, and as they neared it Mr. Webster stood talking to Annie about the time "long, long ago," when she had been rescued by a lifeboat there, and remarking on the curious coincidence that she should happen to come to the same place in distress a second time.

The gale, although somewhat more moderate, was still blowing strong, and an "ugly sea" was rolling on the bank where the *Swordfish* had gone ashore many years before. This, however, mattered little, because the direction of the wind was such that they could steer well clear of it. But the channel leading to the harbour was very sinuous, and, as the pilot observed, required careful steering. In one part this channel was so crooked that it became necessary to go on the other tack a short distance. In ordinary circumstances the captain would have thought nothing of this, but he felt anxious just then, because some of the stores and cordage furnished by mistake to him had been intended for the *Ruby*. Now the *Ruby* was one of the vessels of Webster and Co.

which had been sent away with the hope, if not the intention, that it should be wrecked! The mistake had been discovered only after the *Ocean Queen* had set sail.

"Ready about," cried the pilot.

The men leaped to their respective places.

"Take another pull at that fores'l sheet," said the pilot.

This was done. At sea this would not have been necessary, because the ship was lively and answered her helm well, but in the narrow channel things had to be done more vigorously. The extra pull was given. The tackle of the foresail sheet had been meant for the *Ruby*. It snapped asunder, and the ship missed stays and fell away.

Instantly all was desperate confusion. A hurried attempt was made to wear ship, then two anchors were let go, but almost before the startled owner was aware of what had occurred, the good ship received a shock which made her quiver from stem to stern. She lifted with the next wave, and in another minute was fast on the shoal which had proved fatal to the *Swordfish*, with the waves dashing wildly over her.

Long before this occurred, our hero, Harry Boyns, had been watching the vessel with considerable anxiety. He little knew who was on board of her, else would his anxiety have been infinitely increased. But Harry was one of those men who do not require the spur of self-interest to keep them alive to duty. He had observed that the ship was in distress, and, as the honorary secretary of the Lifeboat Branch, he summoned together the crew of his boat. Thus all was in readiness for action when the disaster occurred to the *Ocean Queen*.

Instantly the lifeboat was run down to the beach, where hundreds of willing hands were ready to launch her, for the people had poured out of the town on the first rumour of what was going on. The crew leaped into the boat and seized the oars. The launching-ropes were manned. A loud "Huzzah" was given, and the lifeboat shot forth on her voyage of mercy, cutting right through the first tremendous billow that met her.

At that time Old Jacob, the coxswain of the boat, happened to be unwell; Harry himself therefore took the steering-oar, and Bob Gaston was in the bow. Mr. Joseph Dowler chanced to be among the spectators on shore. That fussy and conceited individual, conceiving it to be a fitting occasion for the exercise of his tremendous powers, stood upon an elevated rock and began a wildly enthusiastic speech to which nobody listened, and in which he urged the lifeboatmen to do their duty in quite a Nelsonian spirit. Fortunately a sudden gust of wind blew him off his perch. He fell on his head so that his hat was knocked over his eyes, and before he was thoroughly extricated from it, the lifeboat was far from shore, and the men were doing their duty nobly, even although Mr. Dowler's appeal had failed to reach their ears!

It was a tough pull, for wind, waves, and tide combined to beat them back, but they combined in vain. Inch by inch they advanced, slowly and laboriously, although it was so bitterly cold that the men had little feeling in the benumbed hands with which they pulled so gallantly.

At last they reached the vessel, pulled well to windward, cast anchor, and eased off the cable, until they passed her stern and got under her lee. Just then Harry looked up and felt as if he had received a shock from electric fire, for he beheld the pale face of Annie Webster gazing at him with glowing eyes! No longer did he feel the chilling blast. The blood rushed wildly through his veins as he shouted —

"Look alive, Bob, — heave!"

Bob Gaston stood up in the bow, and, with a beautiful swing, cast a line on board, by means of which the boat was hauled alongside. Just at that moment the mainyard came down with a thundering crash upon the ship's deck, fortunately injuring no one. At the same time a tremendous billow broke over the stern of the *Ocean Queen*, and falling into the lifeboat in a cataract completely sunk her. She rose like a cork, keel uppermost, and would have righted at once, but a bight of the mainsail, with some of the wreck, held her down. Her crew, one by one, succeeded in clambering upon her, and Harry shouted to the men in the ship to hand him an axe. One was thrown to him which he caught, and began therewith to cut the wreck of cordage.

"Slit the sail with your knife, Bob Gaston," he cried, but Bob did not reply. All the other men were there; Bob alone was missing. The difficulty of acting in such turmoil is not to be easily estimated. Twenty minutes elapsed before the boat was cleared. When this was accomplished she righted at once, and Bob Gaston was found sticking to the bottom of her, inside, having found sufficient air and space there to keep him alive!

Another moment and Harry Boyns was on the deck of the wreck.

Perhaps the most earnest "Thank God" that ever passed his lips burst from them when he seized Annie's hand and entreated her to go with him at once into the boat.

"Stay! hold!" cried Mr. Webster, seizing Harry wildly by the sleeve and whispering to him in quick earnest tones, "Can nothing be done to save the ship? *All is lost* if she goes!"

"Hold on a minute, lads," cried Harry to the men in the boat; "are the pumps working free, — is your ground tackle good?" he added, turning hastily to the captain.

"Ay, but the men are used up — utterly exhausted."

"Jump aboard, lads," cried Harry to his men.

The men obeyed, leaving four of their number in the boat to keep her off the ship's side. Under Harry's orders some of them manned the pumps, while others went to the windlass.

"Come, boys, make one more effort to save the ship," cried Harry to the fatigued crew; "the tide will rise for another hour, we'll save her yet if you have pluck to try."

Thus appealed to they all set to work, and hove with such goodwill that the ship was soon hauled off the sands — an event which was much accelerated by the gradual abating of the gale and rising of the tide. When it was thought safe to do this, the sails were trimmed, the cables cut, and, finally, the *Ocean Queen* was carried triumphantly into port — saved by the Covelly Lifeboat.

Need we tell you, good reader, that Mr. Webster and his daughter, and Mrs. Niven, spent that night under the roof of hospitable Mrs. Boyns? who — partly because of the melancholy that ever rested like a soft cloud on her mild countenance, and partly because the cap happened to suit her cast of features — looked a very charming widow indeed. Is it necessary to state that Mr. Webster changed his sentiments in regard to young Captain Boyns, and that, from regarding him first with dislike and then with indifference, he came to look upon him as one of the best fellows that ever lived, and was rather pleased than otherwise when he saw him go out, on the first morning after the rescue above recorded, to walk with his daughter among the romantic cliffs of Covelly!

Surely not! It would be an insult to your understanding to suppose that you required such information.

It may be, however, necessary to let you know that, not many weeks after these events, widow Boyns received a letter telling her that Captain Daniel Boyns was still alive and well, and that she might expect to see him within a very short period of time!

On reading thus far, poor Mrs. Boyns fell flat on the sofa in a dead faint, and, being alone at the time, remained in that condition till she recovered, when she eagerly resumed the letter, which went on to say that, after the bottle containing the message from the sea had been cast overboard, the pirates had put himself and his remaining companions — six in number — into a small boat, and left them to perish on the open sea, instead of making them walk the plank, as they had at first threatened. That, providentially, a whale-ship had picked them up two days afterwards, and carried them off on a three years' cruise to the South Seas, where she was wrecked on an uninhabited island. That there they had dwelt from that time to the present date without seeing a single sail — the island being far out of the track of merchant vessels. That at last a ship had been blown out of its course near the island, had taken them on board, and, finally, that here he was, and she might even expect to see him *in a few hours*!

This epistle was written in a curiously shaky hand, and was much blotted, yet, strange to say, it did not seem to have travelled far, it being quite clean and fresh!

The fact was that Captain Boyns was a considerate man. He had gone into a public-house, not ten yards distant from his own dwelling, to pen this letter, fearing that the shock would be too much for his wife if not broken gradually to her. But his impatience was great. He delivered the letter at his own door, and stood behind it just long enough, as he thought, to give her plenty of time to read it, and then burst in upon her just as she was recovering somewhat of her wonted self-possession.

Over the scene that followed we drop the curtain, and return to Mr. Webster, who is once again seated in the old chair in the old office, gazing contemplatively at the portrait of his deceased wife's father.

CHAPTER VIII.

Conclusion.

There are times in the lives, probably, of all men, when the conscience awakes and induces a spirit of self-accusation and repentance. Such a time had arrived in the experience of Mr. John Webster. He had obtained a glimpse of himself in his true colours, and the sight had filled him with dismay. He thought, as he sat in the old chair in the old office, of the wasted life that was behind him, and the little of life that lay, perchance, before. His right hand, from long habit, fumbled with the coin in his trousers-pocket. Taking out a sovereign he laid it on the desk, and gazed at it for some time in silence.

"For your sake," he murmured, "I have all but sold myself, body and soul. For the love of you I have undermined my health, neglected my child, ruined the fortunes of hundreds of men and women, and committed m — "

He could not bring himself to say the word, but he could not help thinking it, and the thought filled him with horror. The memory of that dread hour when he expected every instant to be whelmed in the raging sea rushed upon him vividly. He passed from that to the period of his sickness, when he used to fancy he was struggling fiercely in the seething brine with drowning men — men whom he had brought to that pass, and who strove revengefully to drag him down along with them. He clasped his hands over his eyes as if he thought to shut out those dreadful memories, and groaned in spirit. Despair would have seized upon the gold-lover at that time, had not his guardian angel risen before his agonised mind. Annie's soft tones recurred to him. He thought of the words she had spoken to him, the passages from God's Word that she had read, and, for the first time in his long life, the sordid man of business exclaimed, "God be merciful to me, a sinner!"

No other word escaped him, but when, after remaining motionless for a long time, he removed his hands from his face, the subdued expression that rested there might have led an observer to believe that the prayer had been answered.

A knock at the office-door caused him to start and endeavour to resume his ordinary professional expression and composure as he said, "Come in."

Harry Boyns, however, had not waited for the answer. He was already in the room, hat in hand.

"Now, sir," he said, eagerly, "are you ready to start? The train leaves in half an hour, and we must not risk losing it *to-day*."

"Losing it!" said Mr. Webster, as he rose and slowly put on his greatcoat, assisted by Harry, "why, it just takes me five minutes to walk to the station. How do you propose to spend the remaining twenty-five? — But I say, Harry," he added with a peculiar smile, "how uncommonly spruce you are to-day!"

"Not an unusual condition for a man to be in on his wedding-day," retorted Harry; "and I am sure that I can return you the compliment with interest!"

This was true, for Mr. Webster had "got himself up" that morning with elaborate care. His morning coat still smelt of the brown paper in which it had come home. His waistcoat was immaculately white. His pearl-grey trousers were palpably new. His lavender kid-gloves were painfully clean. His patent-leather boots were glitteringly black, and his *tout ensemble* such as to suggest the idea that a band-box was his appropriate and native home.

"Don't be impatient, boy," he said, putting some books into an iron safe, "I must attend to business first, you know."

"You have no right to attend to business at all, after making it over to me, as you formally did yesterday," said Harry. "If you come here again, sir, and meddle with my department, I shall be compelled to dissolve partnership at once!"

"Please, sir," said Mr. Grinder, appearing suddenly at the door, in a costume which was remarkable for its splendour and the badness of its fit — for Grinder's was a figure that no ordinary tailor could understand, "Captain Daniel Boyns is at the door."

"Send him in," said Webster.

"He won't come, sir; he's afraid of being late for the train."

"Well, well," said Webster, with a laugh, "come along. Are you ready, Grinder?"

"Yes, sir."

"Then, lock the office-door, and don't forget to take out the key."

So saying, the old gentleman took Harry's arm, and, accompanied by Grinder and Captain Boyns senior, hurried to the train; was whirled in due course to Covelly, and shortly after found himself seated at a wedding-breakfast, along with our hero Harry Boyns, and our heroine Annie Webster, who was costumed as a bride, and looked inexpressibly bewitching. Besides these there were present excellent Mrs. Boyns — happily no longer a widow! — and Grinder, whose susceptible nature rendered it difficult for him to refrain from shedding tears; and a bevy of bride's-maids, so beautiful and sweet that it seemed quite preposterous to suppose that they could remain another day in the estate of spinsterhood. Mr. Joseph Dowler was also there, self-important as ever, and ready for action at a moment's notice; besides a number of friends of the bride and bridegroom, among whom was a pert young gentleman, friend of Mr. Dowler, and a Mr. Crashington, friend of Mr. Webster, — an earnest, enthusiastic old gentleman, who held the opinion that most things in the world were wrong, and who wondered incessantly "why in the world people would not set to work at once to put them all right!" Niven, the old nurse, was there too, of course all excitement and tears, and so was Bob Gaston, whose appearance was powerfully suggestive of the individual styled in the ballad, "the jolly young waterman."

Now, it would take a whole volume, good reader, to give you the details of all that was said and done by that wedding-party before that breakfast was over. But it is not necessary that we should go into full details. You know quite well, that when the health of the happy couple was drunk, Annie blushed and looked down, and Harry tried to look at ease, but failed to do so, in consequence of the speech which had cost him such agonising thought the night before, which he had prepared with such extreme care, which contained such an inconceivable amount of sentimental nonsense, which he fortunately forgot every word of at the critical moment of delivery, and, instead thereof, delivered a few short, earnest, stammering sentences, which were full of bad grammar and blunders, but which, nevertheless, admirably conveyed the true, manly sentiments of his heart. You also know, doubtless, that the groom's-man rose to propose the health of the bride's-maids, but you cannot be supposed to know that Dowler rose at the same time, having been told by his pert young friend that he was expected to perform that duty in consequence of the groom's-man being "unaccustomed to public speaking!" Dowler, although not easily put down, was, after some trouble, convinced that he had made a mistake, and sat down without making an apology, and with a mental resolve to strike in at the first favourable opportunity.

When these and various other toasts had been drunk and replied to, the health of Mr. Crashington, as a very old friend of the bride's family, was proposed. Hereupon Crashington started to his feet. Dowler, who was slightly deaf, and had only caught something about "old friend of the family," also started up, and announced to the company that that was the happiest moment of his life; an announcement which the company received with an explosion of laughter so loud and long that the two "old friends of the family" stood gazing in speechless amazement at the company, and at each other for three or four minutes. At last silence was obtained, and Dowler exclaimed, "Sir," to which Crashington replied, "Sir," and several of the company cried, laughingly, "Sit down, Dowler."

It is certain that Dowler would not have obeyed the order, had not his pert young friend caught him by the coat-tails and pulled him down with such violence that he sat still astonished!

Then Crashington, ignoring him altogether, turned to Mr. Webster, and said vehemently —

"Sir, and Ladies and Gentlemen, if this is not the happiest moment of *my* life, it is at least the proudest. I am proud to be recognised as an old friend of the family to which our beautiful bride belongs; proud to see my dear Annie wedded to a man who, besides possessing many great and good qualities of mind, has shown himself pre-eminently capable of cherishing and protecting his wife, by the frequency and success with which he has risked his own life to save the lives of others. But, Ladies and Gentlemen, things more serious than proposing toasts and paying compliments are before us to-day. I regard this as a lifeboat wedding, if I may be allowed the expression. In early life the blooming bride of to-day was saved by a lifeboat, and the brave man who steered that boat, and dived into the sea to rescue the child, now sits on my left hand. Again, years after, a lifeboat saved, not only the bride, but her father and her father's ship; which last, although comparatively insignificant, was, nevertheless, the means of preventing the fortunes of the family from being utterly wrecked, and the man who steered the boat on that occasion, as you all know, was the bridegroom? But — to turn from the particular to the general question — I am sure, Ladies and Gentlemen, that you will bear with me while I descant for a little on the wrong that is done to society by the present state of our laws in reference to the saving of life from shipwreck. Despite the activity of our noble Lifeboat Institution; despite the efficiency of her splendid boats, and the courage of those who man them; despite the vigour and zeal of our coastguardmen, whose working of the rocket apparatus cannot be too highly praised; despite all this, I say, hundreds of lives are lost annually on our coasts which might be saved; and I feel assured that if the British public will continue their earnest support to our great National Institution, this death-roll must continue to be diminished. My friends sometimes tell me that I am a visionary — that many of my opinions are ridiculous. Is it ridiculous that I should regard the annual loss of nearly 600 lives, and above two millions of money, as being worthy of the serious attention of every friend of his country?

"Excuse me if I refrain from inflicting on you my own opinions, and, instead, quote those of a correspondent of the *Times*..."

Here the old gentleman hastily unfolded a newspaper, and read as follows: —

"'Why should not such an amount of information be obtained as will not only induce, but enable the Board of Trade immediately to frame some plain, practical measure, the enforcement of which would tend to lighten the appalling yearly death-list from shipwreck? The plan I would suggest is that the Board of Trade should prepare a chart of the British and Irish coasts, on which every lifeboat, rocket-apparatus, and mortar station should be laid down and along with this a sort of guide-book, with instructions giving every particular connected with them, — such as, their distances from each other, whether they are stationary or transportable, and the probable time that would elapse before one or the other could be brought to work with a view to the rescue of the shipwrecked crew. To illustrate my idea more plainly, I will take the eastern shore of Mounts Bay in Cornwall. A vessel has been driven on shore at Gunwalloe; the captain, having this chart, would find that there is a lifeboat at Mullion, on the south, and a transporting lifeboat at Porthleven, on the north of him, as well as a rocket-apparatus at each place. Referring to his book of instructions, he would find something like this: — "The Mullion lifeboat will drop down on you from Mullion Island. The Porthleven boat will most likely be launched from the beach opposite. All going well, one or other of the boats will be alongside in less than an hour and a half. Look out and get ready for the rocket lines in an hour after striking." The very knowledge even that the means of saving life are at hand would enable the captain to maintain a certain amount of discipline, while passengers and crew alike would retain in a great measure their presence of mind, and be prepared for every emergency. And again, as is often the case, if a captain is compelled to run his ship ashore, with the view of saving the lives intrusted to him, he would at once find from his chart and book of instructions the safest and nearest point from which he could obtain the desired assistance. It should be imperative (not optional, as at present) for every vessel to carry a certain number of lifebelts. The cork jacket recommended by the Royal National Institution is by far the best yet introduced, not only on account of its simplicity and cheapness, but because it affords, also, warmth and protection to the body.'

"Now, Ladies and Gentlemen," continued Crashington earnestly, "here you have the opinions of a man with whom I entirely agree, for, while much is done by philanthropists, too little is done by Government to rescue those who are in peril on our shores. In conclusion, let me thank you, Ladies and Gentlemen, for drinking my health, and permit me also to reiterate my hope that the happy pair who have this day been united may long live to support the lifeboat cause, and never require the services of a lifeboat."

Although Crashington's remarks were regarded by some of the wedding-party as being somewhat out of place, Mr. John Webster listened to them with marked attention, and replied to them with deep feeling. After commenting slightly on the kind manner in which he had referred to the heroic deeds of his son-in-law, and expressing his belief and hope, that, now that he had married Annie, and become a member of the firm of Webster and Co., a life of usefulness and happiness lay before him, he went on to say —

"I heartily sympathise with you, sir, in designating this a lifeboat-wedding, because, under God, my daughter and I owe our lives to the lifeboat. You are also right in stating that the lifeboat has been the means of preserving my fortunes from being wrecked, because the saving of the *Ocean Queen* was a momentous turning-point in my affairs. But a far higher and more blessed result has accrued to myself than the saving of life or fortune, for these events have been made the means of opening my eyes to the truth of God, and inducing me to accept the offer of free forgiveness held out to me by that blessed Saviour to whom my dear Annie has clung for many a year, while I was altogether immersed in business. I feel myself justified, therefore, in saying, with deep humility and gratitude, that *I* have been saved by the lifeboat — body and soul."

www.ingramcontent.com/pod-product-compliance
Lightning Source LLC
Chambersburg PA
CBHW022047170626
46808CB00003B/1393